FLAME AND WARPAINT
A DEATHLESS LOVE NOVEL

ZORA FOX

WELCOME TO THE EIGHT REALMS

A land of gods and goddesses—a savage, beautiful collection of islands in the Corae Sea. The stories here are violent, with explicit sexual content not intended for anyone under 18. These books about deathless love feature dark, often twisted romances. Enter at your own risk.

ZENIA

Ruled by Thenios, God-King of lightning

APHRISO

Ruled by Cytherea, goddess of pleasure

ERISET

Contested land, ruled by Ares and Bellona, god and goddess of war

MENOS

Ruled by Scira, goddess of wisdom

NALIA

Ruled by Basileus, god of the ocean

HYPERION

Ruled by Lox, god of the sun

KANTHAROS

Ruled by Vesta, goddess of hearth and home

FAR REALM

Ruled by Hades, god of the dead

Content warnings for this story of deathless love: murder, blood, references to war, strong language, and explicit sex including BDSM-style scenes

BELLONA

If anything was going to salvage this godsforsaken trip, it was the male with his fingers around my neck. He didn't know the pulse points and the pads of his hand were soft, but he could squeeze hard enough to cut off air. That left only the pound, pound, pound of him between my legs and the feeling of my back scraping along the tabletop.

The documents under me were useless anyway. I'd spent the better part of today studying the records of Thenios' victory against the Terror. He wouldn't lend them—he was so godsdamn stubborn—and I'd memorized all the battle records at home. I thought that *here,* at the site of the Great Victory, I'd find something, some crumb to give me an edge. Even though Arcan handed me parchment after parchment, book after book, none offered a new approach. After almost a full day wasted, I screamed and threw the nearest offending book against the shelves. The Archives were supposed to house knowledge, not vague praise for the victors without explaining how they'd done it.

I adjusted my chin so I could speak. "You weakling," I taunted.

Arcan hardened his grasp. I wasn't easy to dominate in any scenario. Besides being tall and hard with muscle, I had centuries of battle experience. But I let the Archivist try.

His silver eyes in a bronze face made for a pretty view as he moved over me. The hand choking me was attached to robe-covered shoulders broad enough to bear arms if he gave up the Archives. Not that I would ask him.

I had my own war to fight, and besides, we'd only seen each other a couple times in our long lives. In general, I demanded texts and he provided them. Today, however, I wanted more and I could see beneath a veneer of apprehension that he wondered what it would be like to have me too.

So here we were. I did unbuckle several knives at my waist so he could pull down my clothes, but I hadn't even had time to take off my metal fingertips before I let him throw me on this table, yank down my leather pants, and plunge inside me.

I liked the slap of him against me, but release wasn't close. I had to lose control.

"Slap me," I ordered.

His hand came away with some of the black warpaint I always wore streaked across my face.

"Choke me when—" But apparently he understood because he properly choked me right as his grunts and thrusts grew more frantic.

A book fell to the floor. Hopefully the official account of the Great Victory.

The piercing ache of pleasure finally started to build inside me. I wheezed against his hand.

Bold now, Arcan brought his face close to mine. I bared my teeth and bit at him, intentionally missing wide. But at that, just as my own release was cresting, he groaned and pulled out. He came into his robe, probably to spare the books.

I sat up, clipping my knives and other weapons back on, disgusted. The intricate braids woven into the hair I wore long between the shaved sides of my head hadn't even come undone.

Arcan adjusted himself, panting, clearly enjoying more satisfaction than I'd gotten. My wire-sprung anger after a fruitless day here only increased.

I gripped the Archivist by the chin with the sharp metal points of my fingers. "Never leave the queen of war unsatisfied," I snarled, dragging my dangerous nails across his skin. Thin lines of blood appeared. Nothing serious.

His silver eyes went wide, uncomprehending.

He wasn't worth my time. I had bigger worries, like the war over my realm and the audience Thenios demanded with me this evening. If the High King wanted me to help him with another skirmish, so help me, I might blind one of his eyes. No matter that he was my father and the Eight Realms' sovereign. I couldn't bear more of his petty squabbling.

I glanced at the fallen records around the disheveled table, then at Arcan, then marched out to make my meeting with the King.

THIS PLACE WAS SO FAMILIAR. THE SCENT OF HONEY AND mountain air. Gold everywhere. From the tapestries to the stone pillars to the lofted ceilings—everything with my father's symbol of a stylized lightning bolt, of course—each sight brought me back to previous times I'd trod this ground. A thousand memories sliced through my mind: Ares and I play-fighting under massive tables, racing to the tallest overlook, competing in holiday challenges...

Why did so many of my memories have to have *him*? I had other siblings. Lox and Vesta. But they were the good children, the obedient, helpful ones. Ares and I made our own chaos. For a time, we were partners.

I was too young to notice the signs.

Images turned sour then ashy in my mouth. I swallowed thickly and raised my chin. That camaraderie would never be again. I cursed myself for regretting him even for an instant. Traitor.

"Bellona?" I knew the voice like I know my own, the only one I was glad to hear in these halls.

"Mother."

She approached through the abandoned stone hallway with a look of suspicion firmly in place. Mother had three expres-sions—suspicion, anger, and pride.

The first time I'd beaten Ares in an official training ring, I saw the elusive pride. It was hand to hand, a fair fight, without my blast of air or Ares' manipulation of metal. Mother had bet on me against the King, so I gave her a reason to gloat, to further her own cause in a marriage she hated. Even though I knew the reason for that slight smile, I'd chased that sensation ever since.

Or I did until my life because too full of survival to care about anything else. That was generations of humanity ago.

Mother touched my shoulder, her version of an embrace. She was tremendously tall, taller even than I was, with tan skin and blonde hair. I looked nothing like her. When I was young, I'd even asked if I was one of my father's bastard children, but she insisted Ares and I belonged to her.

"I didn't know you were coming." Her words were laced with underlying theories.

"The High King demanded an audience," I replied, barely keeping my scorn at bay.

Her lips moved as though she were sucking the inside of them. "Has he given a reason?"

"He wants my help for something." It was an assumption, but a good one. The High King envied my armies and war skill. He also envied everyone else. In his eyes, I ended up as nothing but a tool.

Mother's eyes grew steely with agreement and she nodded. "You're not staying long, I take it."

"I don't plan to." We both knew I couldn't refuse any command outright without risking eternal banishment and imprisonment, but I'd done my share of maneuvering. If I couldn't refuse, I would negotiate terms until the final result equaled refusal anyway. Negotiation wasn't always my strong suit, but we'd done this dance before. I had a lifetime of experience dealing with my father. "I'm on my way to talk to him now," I said.

Mother drew in a slow breath. "I'll send a cup of spirits to your room in a few hours."

I reached for her hand in thanks, careful not to pierce her

with my metal points. She knew I didn't need much—space, competence, and a stiff drink on days like this.

And I had to get back to my people. They scratched at the edge of my mind, but I couldn't think about them too insistently or rage and fear would choke me more surely than Arcan had. Would they be safe while I was gone?

"I heard about the raid at Euphodia," Mother said gently, like the feathers on an arrow. She set her jaw. On her, the expression looked regal. On me, it would look threatening.

"Four hundred sixteen human casualties," I recited. "Three demi-gods. We got the landing back from him the next day."

"Good." Her elegant brows arched mostly with anger, but I detected a hint of pride.

It wasn't enough to erase the image of the scene I'd encountered two weeks ago. Bloody, mutilated bodies of humans strewn like discarded fish in a market. My healers had only found two clinging to life. They'd both died later. No one to put coins on their eyes and send them to the Far Realm.

The Twin Armies, as citizens of Eriset called my troops and Ares' band of thugs, fought again with the bodies still there. The air stank. Birds and scavenging dogs picked at the dead flesh. Yes, I'd regained the landing, but the drive to destroy my brother was a fire that couldn't be pacified by one victory.

When I stumbled upon a pair of twin children, I gave the healers four coins and told them to send the corpses off. Maybe in the Far Realm they could experience a second life to make up for the miserable one they'd lived in Eriset.

That raid was just one example of why I had to return and could not spare another second for my selfish father. An ache pressed against my ribcage, always there but sometimes subdued enough not to feel painful.

"I'm leaving as soon as I can," I said, "but thank you for that drink."

Mother brought her face closer to mine. No one in Eriset dared to do that. "Give him hell," she said, quiet and distinct.

Whether she meant Ares or Thenios the High King, it didn't matter. I was Bellona, goddess of war, queen of bloodshed, conqueror of cities.

Of course I would give them hell.

❧ 2 ❧

BELLONA

I didn't acknowledge any of the attendants as I stalked into my father's throne room, though I counted them. Twelve. He loved to be surrounded by worshippers and consorts who tended to his every whim. Constantly being waited on had turned his brain selfish and soft.

Guards were for outside this room. Small, naked, un-battled-trained people were for inside. But force of habit made me check.

He sat on the only throne in the room. My mother was no more than an accessory to him, but divine marriages were eternal. Even if she could, she wouldn't leave him, since their alliance prevented Thenios from gaining too much power by coupling as a bid for more territory. Mother stayed in the marriage to spite him as much as anything else.

A practiced smile spread over his bearded face at my entrance. His black hair and beard were both streaked with white. His skin, paler than my mother's, matched mine. Ares had inherited Mother's coloring and I'd only gotten her dark eyes.

I glared at the High King.

"Bellona!" he greeted, spreading his arms. He still wore long, dusty blue robes that had been the fashion centuries ago. He maintained they were more regal. The style hadn't completely died away because of those who wanted to mirror him. I thought they looked ridiculous. One of his nipples was showing.

"Father."

"You still wear your hair that way?"

My eyes narrowed. "You still stick your dick in anything that moves?"

His smile wobbled, then fit back in place. "You speak to your mother too much."

I stopped at the foot of the throne. We peered eye to eye. "What do you want?"

"Bellona. Daughter. Why do you assume the worst of me?" Finally, I saw a flash in his blue eyes. I preferred anger over this posturing.

"I assume nothing. Experience had led me to predict patterns. Now, what do you want?"

"I want to talk."

Approaching from behind the throne, a female nymph, totally nude, handed him a drink. Her eyes flicked warily to me. The servants still acted dreamily attentive, as usual, but my presence obviously made them nervous.

"So you summoned me?" I didn't hide my skepticism. "Why not Lox, Vesta...?" I almost added Ares to the list.

Father loved him. Even after everything my brother had done while he looked passively on.

"You're capable, Bellona," he said, adjusting his sitting position. "But you're under strain. I want to know how you fare."

"Wonderfully." Father had never offered to help my cause before and he wouldn't begin now. I didn't avert my gaze from his. Every nerve in my body felt tight. That ache behind my breastbone increased.

Thenios sighed. "The issue of limited land drives us to violence."

My lips thinned in disagreement.

"You and Ares are both so powerful that you deserve your own realms." He cast his eyes up wistfully. "The Nine Realms. Can you envision it?" When he met my eyes, there was almost a challenge in the look, as if he had correctly read my mind, that giving Ares his own Realm was bullshit.

I waited, feet spread apart and planted, hands at my sides.

He sipped at his drink. Thenios' throne room was massive and circular, a place for many to gather, though now it just held an impressive bevy of servants, the High King, and me.

His tone shifted from cajoling to businesslike. "I've recently heard rumors of the Beyond in turmoil, longing for a permanent leader, for order." He gestured one pale hand toward me. A blue and silver ring winked on his finger.

"Those rumors aren't new," I replied. They'd persisted for several decades, since the earthquake. I hadn't cared then. I didn't care now.

Eriset and Eriset only had been my concern for so long that I only knew two languages. With a life as long as mine, that wasn't something to brag about. The politics of nations outside the Eight Realms reached far past my interest.

"Wars," he continued, leaning forward and twirling the stem of his golden cup in two fingers. "Confusion. Incompetent gods."

My spine prickled at that. He knew how to nettle me. That scenario was exactly what I longed to step into, to remedy. I curled my lip. "The Beyond is vast. I won't abandon my people to chase a meaningless conquest."

"Not meaningless. Not meaningless." His deep voice echoed through his cavernous chest, making even soft words loud.

So this was his game. I didn't feel equipped to be diplomatic. Thenios wanted more land to rule, so he'd send me to subdue them.

"Meaningless to me," I said. "They have the old gods, don't they? Let them deal with those problems." I didn't know much about the old gods of the north—we hadn't interacted in centuries—but they had big castles, impressive legacies, etc., etc. They had to be good for something.

He sat back again. "And if they can't?"

I exhaled through gritted teeth. "Then *you* help them, if you feel so strongly."

"Don't be heartless, Bellona!"

I laughed mirthlessly. "I, heartless? You're the one who—"

"Basileus' ships encountered a raft last month. A human family of six was attempting to survive on it as they journeyed from the Beyond to the Eight Realms." He reached behind him and produced a tiny carved dog.

My gut churned to see him hold it up alongside the goblet. The farce of it. The godsdamned farce.

Attempting to survive. Not succeeding, then. The great seas around the Realms weren't kind, especially to humans.

I snatched the figure, just so I didn't have to face that image anymore. My father's lecherous fingers had no right to hold this toy, if it even was what he implied. The edges of the wooden ears dug into my palm.

I hated the smug look on Father's face. "See?" he said. "This isn't an imaginary problem. The unrest is one we can solve."

"I never said it was imaginary. I said it wasn't my problem. Eriset is more than enough already."

He hadn't commanded anything of me yet. I paid close attention to his language. So far, I'd been defiant but hadn't overstepped the king enough to be punished harshly.

"If this is all you wanted," I said, "you could have sent a message."

"I did. To you and your brother."

That gave me pause. My heart pounded thickly with wariness.

This was just like Thenios. He was so removed from the realities of war that he liked to stoke our conflict as a sort of sibling competition, a show of his own strength in some fucking misguided way, not as a series of blood-soaked massacres that I couldn't always prevent. My brother was greedy, violent, and childishly impulsive. And strong. His armies were among the most well-equipped in the world. I'd depleted my stores at the beginning by paying for passage across the water for the human slain. In retrospect, it was sentimental idiocy, but at the time, that decision had helped me bear one day to the next. Either I was tougher now or else I couldn't remember anything but this state of constant tension.

I resisted the urge to rub at the pain in my chest.

"What did Ares say to your proposition?" I could imagine him jumping at the chance to conquer more lands. If he didn't regularly fuck Queen Cytherea, he'd already have tried conquering her island between Eriset and my father's stronghold of Zenia.

Father took a drink. "He's considering it."

Ares didn't consider. He acted.

I weighed the pros and cons if Ares did act on my father's plan. Getting him out of Eriset for any length of time was a benefit to me. But if he did conquer the nearest landmass of the Beyond, that would give him more power.

And our definitions of conquering weren't the same.

For him, it meant carving a bloody wound through the heart of the land. For me, it meant taking the necessary actions to establish dominance. I accepted violence—gladly, it was true— but he relished it. No one would be safe.

I squeezed the little dog in my fist. It was useless pondering hypothetical scenarios. Maybe Father never contacted Ares at all.

At home, I had to counter real threats and save citizens of the land I actually ruled.

Distraction meant death.

"Then Ares can consider it," I said. "I'm not interested."

The High King's gaze dipped to my white knuckles closed around the toy. "I'll give you time to see the sense in what I propose. I'd even enforce a truce while you were gone."

My brows lowered. He'd never offered to intervene before.

"I know you care about your humans."

My throat worked. How did he know just what strings to tug? I couldn't believe I was considering his offer.

The simple awareness of that fact brought me back to myself. "You could have done that a long time ago," I spat. With the slightest of required bows, I pivoted and practically ran out of that cursed room to find the liquor Mother had promised.

3

BELLONA

I shouldn't have stayed the extra night, but after one cup of liquor (the High Court had the best) I ordered another from a servant and then a third before I fell asleep angry.

My armies would stand vigilant against attack when I wasn't there, but I knew from experience that their discipline atrophied quickly without swift consequences. As if the threat of death by Ares' forces wasn't enough of a consequence.

I rubbed the aching spot on my chest before I gathered my knives, buckled them on one by one, tucked one into my braid, checked the clasp on my metal arm cuff for the tiny compartment there.

Conquering an area of the Beyond wouldn't solve my problem. Ares didn't just need more land. He needed to be stopped for good, thrown to the farthest reaches of the world where no living beings stood in his bloody way. We couldn't peacefully exist in separate realms. Our fight wasn't over territory. It would be eternal war unless I destroyed him.

So no, I wouldn't bow to my father's wishes. He could wheedle or scream or bribe all he wanted.

I glared at his lightning symbol etched into the table where I'd found the cup Mother sent me. Wrenching out a blade from my hip, I carved it out and replaced it with my own—a simple torch.

It was time to get back to Eriset.

Gathering my energy, I focused on the inner rooms of my primary fortress. Filaments of thought reached forward through the intervening space between the room where I stood and the place I wanted to travel. I closed my eyes. It was a long way to go in one jump, but a familiar path. I knew the fall from here to the fortress along that thought-forged path would take a beat too long. It would make my insides clench, my breath stall, and a shout build in my entire body before... landing at home.

I exhaled heavily and straightened. A dozen soldiers straightened and saluted.

Torches resembling my symbol burned hot in rows along the wall, gleaming off the armor and polished leather. Even so, this low-ceilinged room was dark, almost black.

I ignored the guards who had waited for me and prowled upstairs. I needed news. I needed to know that Ares hadn't done anything especially stupid while I was gone.

"Fetch Lagus," I ordered at the top of the stairs. "I'll be in the war council."

The war council was a chamber on the main floor of the fortress, meant for joint meetings, but I usually went there alone. It housed some of the most complete maps, tactical charts and lists, as well as schematics for potential new weapons.

Certain metals catered to my brother's ability. He could control them as if they were made of water, turn them against us.

I liked the old weapons best—the simple, satisfying slice of a knife—but I'd use whatever means necessary to upend my brother's tyranny. We'd made strides in the laboratories I hid on the far side of my territory. These excellent pointed gauntlets, for instance.

I stood to the side by a stone pillar. The whole fortress was stone. Safer that way. Around me were rows of benches and desks, documents and maps.

I still gripped the knife I'd used to erase my father's symbol. Angling it, I drew it along the stone to resharpen the point. The scraping of the metal, the repetitive movement, soothed me. I loved an effective blade.

That was how Lagus found me, running my knife against the large column. Lagus oversaw this week's watch in Strayhill. Lately, Ares had been pushing hard against that territory, so I needed an update. I paused at his approach, testing the point of the knife against the underside of one finger. Ruby blood welled instantly.

"Report," I said.

"Welcome back, my queen."

Lagus was a minor demi-god, observant, with honey-glass eyes and ill-advised earrings that dangled too far down. He pursed his lips thin. I always thought it unusual that his lips were the same color as the rest of his skin. Why he was making that face, though, was the immediate question.

"What?" I demanded.

"Your commanders needed to send more troops to Strayhill in your absence."

"Why?" There should have been plenty. I'd personally ordered two extra regiments to swell their numbers while I was gone.

"It wasn't the troops they needed so much as the commander with them."

Why wouldn't this idiot get to the point? I squeezed the hilt of my knife.

"General Methon has been killed."

I inhaled sharply. General Methon was one of the best human commanders in my army. A man I could trust. "How did that happen? There should have been watchmen overlapping every hour. You know Ares thinks Strayhill is vulnerable. Without my presence, the watch was doubled!"

At his hesitation, I squinted at him through my warpaint. "Wasn't it?"

His throat worked. "The message was still en route when we got the news about the general's death."

"En route," I repeated, taking a step forward. "The message should have been sent as soon as I left."

"It was only a few hours later that I sent it to the front, but then—"

I lashed out, grabbing one of his long earrings, and ripping it out. "You sent it when?"

"Only a few hours after you left," he gasped, his hand flying to his bloody ear.

"Leaving everyone there in danger. You can praise the

Divine that only the general was killed and not the whole gods-damned army!" I leaned close, catching the coppery scent of blood, which sent my head spinning. "I know how my brother works." At my side, the blade gleamed sharp and ready.

Lagus' heart pounded visibly in his chest. His shaky breathing warmed my cheek. I took in a lungful of his smell. I had compassion for my subjects, but none for fools. Curse me, but I could get high on the smell of the blood and fear of my enemies.

And right now, Lagus was my enemy.

"Do *you* know how Ares works?" I persisted.

I licked my lips. He didn't dare answer.

"You cost a man his life."

When he finally opened his mouth again, I pulled out his slimy tongue. He tried to pull it back in, but I cut it out, fast as thought.

He screamed, blood dribbling freely from his mouth.

"Your only payment is your voice, since you can't seem to remember what to say. Go."

Holding his face, he ran from the room. His severed tongue lay on the ground. I kicked it aside. It truly was a miracle that more lives hadn't been lost. I couldn't afford to have overseers like Lagus. My mouthpiece needed to say the right fucking things at the right fucking times.

I stepped out of the room to order that all the rest of the territorial overseers meet me immediately. Hopefully there weren't any more disasters.

Still, I was angry enough at the events of the past day that cutting out another tongue didn't sound so terrible. The only bright side was the confirmation that this metal alloy worked just as well as steel.

GENERAL MATHON HADN'T JUST BEEN KILLED, HE'D BEEN eviscerated. The report was brief, but brutal: *Identified by a freckle on his index finger after that piece was cleaned.* My brother loved blood, liked the pain of his victims. I would have recognized Ares' signature in the state of the general's body even if I'd found it in Zenia.

Strayhill had new leadership in place now, but I disliked sifting through human soldiers to find generals. Even the good ones didn't last. In a realm where the gods were at war, humans were always the first casualties.

Luckily, no other strongholds had been breached. Besides a tiny skirmish near the eastern shoreline, Ares had caused no more chaos. He hadn't gained a foot of ground.

I clacked my metal fingertips together. That shouldn't count as lucky. I was gone for two days. Not even two days.

"My queen." The new general knelt and bowed his head before me, long hair pulled back in a light brown tail. Even standing, he was half a head shorter than me. The place where he knelt had been cleaned of Lagus' blood.

"Speak," I said, setting aside the new maps I'd been presented. More detail had been filled in around the edges. Maps of the Eight Realms didn't include the entire island that belonged to Hades. It only showed a corner of it on the top left of the map. More complete charts showed Hades' realm to be the largest by far, but fear kept most people from going.

A few years into my conflict with Ares, I asked Hades to join my cause but he refused. Our relationship was civil, but I had the feeling he begrudged the extra work I laid on his country by sending over so many corpses.

I doubted even Hades could give General Mathon a second life.

"Patrols have been doubled, as you requested."

"As a temporary measure," I cut in.

"Yes, my queen. When we gain more intelligence, the additions will respond to any newer threats." He didn't raise his head.

"Keep me informed. You may go."

Keeping his eyes down, he rose, pounded the torch symbol above his heart with a fist, and left.

Alone, I sighed. Humans for generations knew war, prepared for war, died at war. I didn't want to be the goddess of eternal war only, but also the goddess of victory. This conflict belonged to me and Ares, not all these soldiers and civilians. I'd gladly eat my brother's heart if I thought he would die from it. The fantasy was a familiar one. Frankly, I'd eat his heart anyway if I could get close enough to him to do it. Gods couldn't die, but they could be tortured.

I tapped my fingertips on the map. Eight Realms, with Hades' as the largest, and beyond... Few knew what lay in the Beyond, due north. The nearest land mass appeared to be a continent as expansive as the Far Realm. The cryptic name Urd was scrawled there. Apart from the shoreline, the interior was devoid of detail. Empty.

Incompetent gods. Wars. Infighting.

A muscle ticked in my cheek. Thenios said he would enforce a truce on Eriset if I went. A truce would mean no killing of opposing armies or subjects...

Heat built in my neck. I couldn't be considering his offer. I couldn't be. Going to the Beyond would be a small bandage on a gaping wound. While I was busy, Ares would have time to plan his next attack.

I plucked my pointer finger from the tabletop where I'd stabbed a hole in Urd.

Heaving measured breaths through my nose, I stared at the empty map. Suddenly resolved, I stood.

It was exhausting to travel that far through the air twice in one day, but I had to see my father one more time. I needed his promise and the exact terms of the truce he would enforce. I needed the hell he'd rain on Ares if he failed to honor it.

And if he gave me all that, I'd finally give my people the respite they deserved.

I'd tame the Beyond.

4

TYR

The eyes of all the assembled gods watched me as I stood before Hrafnir's throne in the Great Hall. Had this meeting been called just for me? I bet it had.

Hrafnir's one eye—sacrificed to become leader among the old gods—glared shrewdly. I thought back on my week, but there were too many things I knew he could criticize to choose one. I'd done what I had to, and that had to be enough for me.

Two ravens perched on the wings of his wooden throne, cocking their heads. Their attention was so focused, I couldn't decide if I thought they were just devoted animals or really gods in disguise.

Ever since I was a child (hell, ever since my grandparents were children), the story of Hrafnir's spying ravens passed between us in whispers. We'd start by bowing our foreheads to the hearth and asking Hrafnir for blessings, but as we wrapped ourselves in furs and settled in to eat some thin stew in front of the wood fire, stories would flow. Spying ravens, lost eyes, sacred wells, mysterious runes...

I'd thought Hrafnir would be better in person.

"Are you on the side of humans?" the king began, his voice commanding.

So that was what this was about. "I'm on the side of not being an asshole."

One of the goddesses gasped at my insolence. At the beginning, I wouldn't have spoken like that to a god I used to worship, but now I saw Hrafnir was a lot like us. He let pride blind his other eye to the reality of what was really happening in Urd. His betrayal of that image of a just ruler I'd pictured as a boy stirred up my frustration until I couldn't hide how pissed off I was. This day was already tough enough without having to listen to old gods acting superior.

"Jotar burned two human homes with people inside," I explained. "He deserved to lose the arm that did it."

"And now," Hrafnir continued, "he will have to live eternally without it."

"Hopefully not." We hadn't figured out if there was a way for gods to die. Unsurprisingly, no one had volunteered to try it out.

"Jotar!" Hrafnir's shout acted as a reprimand to me.

Jotar rose from his place near part of the wall carved like the twisting tree of creation. The entire round, wooden room had lots of carvings like that. They were impressive, but didn't all go together. Artisans had given their services as offerings to the old gods when they arrived. But there had been so much turmoil—there still *was* so much turmoil—that the hall looked grandly unfinished. Every time I stepped in here, the reminder stood out. Now about fifteen gods, old and new, lined the room.

Jotar moved to stand beside me. I could practically feel the heat of his rage against my bare side. This meeting had been called suddenly and it was hot outside, so I looked more savage than the rest without my shirt, black tattoos on full display.

Breaking off his murderous stare and half-whispered threats, Jotar ran his remaining hand over his beard, a less distinguished version of Hrafnir's, before he could collect himself to speak. "The humans had encroached on sacred land and both their fathers had fought—"

"Their fathers, not themselves!" I interrupted.

"—against us in the war. *And* the families had both been hoarding resources from over the border."

I ground my teeth. Gods weren't the only ones with a right to resources, even if we did live longer.

Peace. Could no one understand the word?

Jotar gained no sympathy from me, despite the stained bandages wrapping the stump of his left arm.

"Humans have a right to exist," I said.

Hrafnir raised his hand imperiously. One of the ravens flapped. "Don't forget, Tyr, that I made you peacekeeper for your skills. Use them wisely. Any punishment to the gods will rebound on your head in the years to come."

I heard the implication: *Humans matter less.* Punishment is appropriate for humans overstepping their bounds but not for arrogant gods.

Jotar shot me a poisonous glare. I met it coolly but inside, I was aflame. Justice wasn't justice if it only applied to us. I'd killed plenty of humans, but as soon as I extended my methods to the gods, they called a bloody meeting about it. By trying to be fair, I was creating enemies that would hate me for centuries. Well, better that than the alternative.

"Then let it rebound," I replied.

"HE'S GETTING TOO BIG," HILD SNAPPED, CRADLING THE CUP of strong tea in her gnarled hands. Her sharp glare slid from Fen my Banewolf, who looked too satisfied to have licked her cup, up to me.

"No such thing," I said, scratching behind his gray ears, now the size of my hands, which were not small. Sitting, Fen almost reached my chest. When I'd found him as a puppy, hunters had cornered him, ready for the kill. Grown Banewolves needed killing. They were savage, breaking people and swallowing them in two terrible bites. But when I'd looked at Fen, I figured a tame Banewolf could be a boon, not a threat. He was still a little wild but he listened to me. Maybe because I was a little wild too.

"You would say that." Hild took a sip from her tea. "You spoil him." The ghost of a smirk passed her lips. Even lined with age, her face made just the same expressions as when we were twenty-five.

That was fifty years ago.

"You two are the only ones I spoil," I responded. "If I didn't, who would care about me?"

Hild scoffed. "The women."

That earned a laugh from me. "What women?"

She sat straighter, setting her cup down. Fen looked so intensely at it that she moved it to the opposite side of the table. "The young women. The ones who look at you and see a god they want to bed."

"Hild..."

"Don't lie to me." Her voice was crackly but her spirit the same. "You were beautiful even *before*."

"Before I became a brutal monster." I heard what people said. I saw the tears in their eyes or the weapons in their hands when I came near. These moments with Hild—secret though they were—provided my only sanctuary.

"You're not a brutal monster. They're fools," she said. "Fools deserve what you give them."

Her words, especially coming from a human, poured like salve into my chest. "They weren't all fools," I revised.

Her voice got quieter and her eyes deepened in their sockets. "These are bad times." She gripped her tea again in both hands—hands that could string a bow faster than I could at one time. A slurp of the strong tea seemed to revive her. "The young women—yes, I hear them talking—still comment when they see you. Indecent things."

I chuckled. "Like what?"

"You'd have an old lady relate these things to you?" She quirked a brow.

"Oh, please. I'd have *Hild* relate them. Besides, I know you have a dirty mind. You've probably said more than half of what you've heard."

Her smile confirmed my suspicions. In a prim voice, she said, "They want to know if the tattoos extend to your cock."

"Did you tell them?"

She smacked my arm, her hand tiny against my bicep. Sometimes I forgot the differences between us.

I was a god. She was human.

I was young. She was old.

As a god, I'd even grown taller. She, on the other hand, had shrunk. Her mind was still sharp, but it hurt to see her sometimes. She never matched my expectation of the bright, tough young woman who had been my best friend. Besides one drunken night, we'd never been lovers. Instead, she had fought by my side, was my confidant. After the earthquake, we'd still managed to support each other through the violent changes. Hild found a wife named Astrid and I fell into my role as peacekeeper. It turned out that keeping the peace more often meant killing or maiming to make a point. I was good at it. I would do what few others could stomach, but it gained me no friends. As long as I had Hild and Fen, I'd be all right. But how long would that be?

A noise outside shook me from my thoughts. Hild's small home lay on the border of human land, near the natural crack formed by the earthquake. Few dared to live so close to the new gods. This area was too often a battle ground. Hatred erupted almost daily, though the brunt of the initial wars had ceased.

I cast Hild a dark look. She had heard it too. A cry of pain.

I jumped up—my head nearly touching the ceiling—and whistled for Fen. In an instant, the small ax Peacekeeper was in my hands. "Stay here," I told Hild. "Thanks for tea."

I didn't like to emerge from Hild's house when anyone could see. She'd already been targeted a couple times for fraternizing with me. I enjoyed every second of destroying the ones who dared to threaten her.

Now, who were these people?

I ducked out of her little house, gripping the handle of my weapon. Fen trotted at my side.

"What's this?" I asked with lethal calm, absorbing the scene in front of me.

Vali, part of the Council of Gods, a good soldier but an insufferable man, led a man and a woman roughly by the back of their collars past where I stood.

The god paused and cast me a self-important look. "These two dipped into the sacred spring. Their filth sullied the waters." He shook the pair. The man, who was taller, only came up to Vali's neck.

"Where are you taking them now?"

"Where do you think?"

"I asked a question." I lowered my voice dangerously. Gods and humans constantly needed to be checked, held back, and the Council had the gall to criticize my methods. My solutions were working, but I still had to fight for every crumb of respect.

"The fields," he answered. The woman's mouth fell open in horror. The man didn't seem to know what to fear more: me or the imminent death Vali threatened.

The fields. The site of the bloodiest battle between humans and gods. It had happened ten years after the earthquake and even now the memory felt fresh. I understood the hatred in their eyes. In the disaster, we had become tall, strong, immortal. They had lost friends and family. What separated gods from mortals was utterly arbitrary. No wonder they were bitter.

But I couldn't let our country rip itself apart. Either every human would die at the hand of the gods, or only those who shredded the peace. Most days I felt like I held up a dam with a thousand holes. But it was still better than wholesale slaughter. This just meant that I did most of the necessary slaughtering.

I approached the couple slowly. "You entered the sacred spring?" I asked.

The man swallowed visibly. "No. We were only—"

Vali let go to cuff him in the head. "We caught them," he explained.

They didn't look wet. Must have just gotten close then. "No one takes that water," I said. Beside me, Fen let out a low growl, sensing my mood. The couple trembled.

I gestured for Vali to let them go. Reluctantly, he obeyed, but the god's eyes still shone with anticipation for the kill.

I flourished Peacekeeper. The man and woman flinched, and I slung it in the loop at my belt. "No one takes that water," I repeated. "Come to the Godlands again and I will personally slit your throats. Go."

"But..." Vali protested.

The water of the sacred spring held untold power. Something in it connected us to the divine and we hadn't figured out how. Humans had died touching it. One human had become a god. We couldn't risk the chaos of having mortals flock to the waters to become one of us. It was too dangerous, too unpredictable.

The couple fled in the direction of more human settlements. Once they disappeared through the trees, I turned my full attention to Vali. "How did they get past the guards?" I demanded.

"They were still returning to their posts after the Council assembly."

"That was over an hour ago. Did they stop for cups?" *They*. I kept saying *they* when it should have been *you*. "Get back to your post, Vali."

"These stupid humans, crawling like bugs over everything," he muttered, glaring in the direction the two had gone.

Fen gave a half-bark, half-growl that stopped him short.

I took a deep breath to stop myself from grabbing his neck and shoving him against the nearest pine. There were enough stories of my impulsivity when the pressure grew too great. Besides, despite my disgust, I needed Vali as an ally. I slowed my words. "Get back to your post."

Too slowly, Vali complied, looking like he'd rather spit on my boots. I'd robbed him of bragging rights, called him out for a shoddy job at the spring, taken over his authority.

Shame that he couldn't age out of my life instead.

5

BELLONA

I crashed into my father's throne room.

His shocked expression betrayed how little he thought I'd take his deal. "Bellona, you know you can't—"

"How long would you honor a truce if I went to the Beyond?"

With a sigh, he sat back again, waving away an attendant who had approached him with something on a platter. Too bad he found his composure so fast. I liked seeing him flustered. "Ah, so you have come around to the obvious benefits of my idea."

I tensed. "I wouldn't put it like that. How long?"

"Careful, daughter." A flash of anger lit his eyes. I'd finally gotten close to his limit for disrespect.

I tried to calm myself, but calm wasn't easy for me. Had I ever felt calm in my life? "If I do this," I said in a tone with fewer barbs, "what would be the terms of the truce you'd uphold while I was gone?"

Thenios peaked his fingers. He enjoyed this far too much. *I never should have returned.* "The standard set of rules. He would be forbidden to attack anyone under your protection."

I bit my tongue to keep myself from cutting in for clarification.

"Similarly, your armies couldn't fight either. To break the truce would mean consequences."

I couldn't hold back anymore. "What consequences?"

"The Far Realm, probably. Abaddon."

Hades' god-prison. The only thing Ares feared. "I want assurances."

He gave me an evaluating look. "What assurances do you seek?"

"Pain, if he hurts my armies or my subjects, divine or human."

"Pain?" His fingers laced. "You'd wish pain on your brother?"

My eyelids fluttered with disbelief. How could he be so unaware of the pain he'd caused me and my people in the past centuries? No, he knew. He just didn't think it important. "Yes," I answered simply.

"He'd have to agree to the terms. You would both stand before me and—"

"I know." I hated to contemplate the two of us in the same room, while I had to stand silent, unable to finish him.

His eyes narrowed at my interruption. "You think he'll agree?"

"If you wish it." I didn't think Ares would want a truce, but I knew he'd obey Thenios if given a direct order. We all would.

My answer seemed to please him. This was as close to diplomacy as I got.

"Please," I continued, "I need a promise that you'll uphold a truce for as long as it takes for me to conquer the Beyond."

A small smile flitted over his features. "You are Bellona, goddess of war. Surely that will not take you very long."

"War isn't one swift killing," I replied. "It's restoring order. You said the Beyond needed order."

"So I did. So I did."

Laughable that he still considered sending *me*. Obviously, order wasn't his first priority.

"And I need the terms of the truce in advance before I agree. Banishment and pain are what I request should either side violate your command." Mine wouldn't. I'd threaten greater punishment even than my father would give. Ares or no one would break the truce. At best, peace—artificial peace, but still—would reign for a time in Eriset. At worst, Ares would attack and suffer consequences beyond what I could rain upon him with my armies.

This idea sounded better all the time.

"I would send any offending party to the farthest reaches of the Far Realm, to Abaddon, should they disobey my word."

"For as long as I am gone in the Beyond."

"Yes, for as long as you are gone."

My heart skipped. This was working. My father was actually stepping in. I'd stopped asking many years ago because of his apathy, his pretend magnanimity when he claimed to let us sort out our own differences. Now, because of his greed, I saw a sliver of hope. Or, if not hope, then something like rest.

"I want to do this immediately," I said.

Thenios chuckled. "Wait, Bellona! I have stipulations too. It is not you who rule the Eight Realms, but I."

My blood cooled. What stipulations?

He seemed to relish my discomfort, though I let none of it show on my face, because he paused for an unnaturally long time. His gaze drifted lazily from me to one of the naked attendants near me. I flexed my jaw with disgust and impatience.

"When you win this savage land for the Eight," he finally resumed, "who will be their leader?"

I didn't care. Let them govern themselves for all I cared. What I wanted was a free Eriset so I could turn my attention to more worthwhile wars, ones that were winnable. My best soldiers would go with me and crush the evil throughout the Realms. Even my dreams of violence felt restful compared to the constant, senseless fight I waged with my own twin.

"You can rule the new land as their queen goddess and Ares can rule Eriset."

A bitter laugh erupted from me. "You think I'll give Eriset to my brother?"

"Won't you? The Beyond is probably much more vast."

"I don't care how vast it is. I wouldn't abandon Eriset for the other seven Realms."

As his pause lengthened, I sensed a storm brewing behind his still exterior. I braced myself. After I'd burst into his throne room uninvited, refused his offers, and cut off his speech, *this* couldn't be the thing I'd get punished for, was it?

"You will." His voice was uncharacteristically quiet. "I'm tired of your attitude of insurrection. You may have insurrection, but at my command. I will only enforce a truce with Ares if you remain in the Beyond to serve as its queen and become the ninth Realm."

My brow furrowed hard, and I had to force air in and out of my lungs. It took everything in me not to charge at him. If anyone else had said those words, he'd already be dead.

It wasn't a truce my father was offering, then. It was victory to Ares while I was sent away to a fucking backwater to increase my father's territories.

"Do you still want to summon him?" the High King prompted.

I didn't think I could control my rage if Thenios summoned Ares right now. The ache in my chest was so piercing I had trouble thinking straight.

With the Beyond in addition to my armies, which were still mine during the truce, damn it, would that finally be enough to tip the scales of the war? Could I find a loophole in my father's plan and be an absentee goddess to Urd in the Beyond? Could I still win back Eriset?

I ran back through my father's words. He hadn't given a command that Ares rule Eriset—thank the divine—but I didn't want to press him yet.

After a few more labored breaths, I released my hands, which had clenched into hard fists. "Yes, summon him."

This was a risk, but it might work.

As long as I managed not to rip my brother to pieces.

"You look like you're apt to explode, Bellona. Relax, this will be good for all of us." The High King called over one of the only clothed servants in the room, a white-pale demi-god named Asper. He wore the same stupid robes as my father, hopelessly out of date. After a few words whispered in his ear, the servant stepped into the air, his long white hair the last part to disappear.

"It will take part of an hour," my father continued, sitting back luxuriously in his chair. "Take the time to calm yourself."

It wasn't a suggestion. I twitched a bow and strode from the room.

Calm myself. Never advice that I took well, or at all.

Maybe I could try to dull my edges. If any part of my idiotic plan was going to work, I had to resist chopping my brother into fine pieces with my claws. That kind of thing would get me sent off to Abaddon faster than thinking.

I exhaled. The only way to resist that temptation was to take off the metal gauntlets.

I'd wait until the last moment. They were my signature, my comfort. Many a traitor and enemy had been sliced by these fingertips.

Too bad Arcan couldn't give a good fuck. That might at least dull the pain behind my breastbone or let me breathe better while Ares was in the room. No time to find someone new. Most were too afraid to fuck me anyway.

I would be.

In the end, I settled for downing two glasses of the strongest spirits I could find. I was reaching for a third when the word came.

Ares was here.

The liquor in my gut curdled. This was a mistake. This was a godsdamned mistake.

Fuck fuck fuck.

My metal gauntlet crushed the cup in my hand, denting the silver. I hurled it at the messenger, who swiftly closed the door.

Sucking in air, I leaned on the table in front of me. Black rage surrounded me like a haze. I hadn't seen my brother in five years. If that time had been fifty, this reunion still would have come too soon.

A truce...

The idea seemed pathetic now. How had I fallen for it? Thenios would never uphold a real truce, one that would allow me to return to Eriset.

I straightened, lifted my chin.

No one would make me cower. Others cowered before me, but no one—not even my evil brother—would make me bow in weakness.

Deliberately, I undid the clasps that held my metal fingertips in place. Easing off one gauntlet, I drew my bare fingertip down the bridge of my nose, where I knew I still had plenty of warpaint. I streaked the black from the middle of my lower lip to the bottom of my chin. The face of war.

Let Ares tremble. I never would.

Heartbeat crashing, I headed back toward the throne room. I should have talked to Mother, told her what was happening. Her commiseration might have helped me steel myself to face my brother again.

I swallowed bile as I pushed past the servants and opened the double doors myself.

There he was.

His hateful shape blocked part of the throne like a rip in space. Something unholy.

I squeezed the gauntlet in my hand. I'd only taken off one.

Ares wore his hair shorn close to the skull, with a dusting of beard. He wore brown leather that crossed over his chest in an X. Gouts of red paint smeared his face and thickly muscled bare arms. A massive sword swung at his side. Bloodbringer. I'd seen enough of that sword to hate it too. It was like my brother, huge and fatal and brainless.

He peered over his shoulder at me, gaze dipping to the metal glove in my hand. One side of his mouth twitched. I stared back at him, choked with memories of the dead and dying, of broken promises and horrific rampages. That he had the gall to stand there without pleading for mercy from me almost left me shaking. But I bit my tongue—literally, I tasted my own blood—and approached the throne.

This had better fucking work.

Thenios looked at the two of us appreciatively, as though we weren't the two of the most dangerous beings in the Eight Realms. If I didn't hate my brother to my very core, Ares and I together could overthrow even the High King. But now, our father looked almost placid. We were not the same twins who left the palace all those centuries ago. Thenios should know that better than most.

"Bellona's surrendering?" Ares drawled, breaking the silence.

"Fuck you!" I lashed out with my remaining metal nails, drawing bloody lines near his elbow.

My brother merely smiled.

"No," Thenios said, flashing me a warning look. "She's conquering the Beyond. Their uncivilized chaos has gone on long enough. Becoming part of the Realms will benefit them as much as it does us."

"So she's running off to do what you say," Ares said.

I could barely breathe through my fury.

"Someone must do it. Who better than our Conqueror of Cities?" Thenios gestured idly toward me.

For the first time, Ares betrayed annoyance. He was like a fire, mindlessly destructive. So explosive that the slightest provocation could ignite him. I felt the heat rise beneath his bronze skin.

I'd earned the title of Conqueror, not him. He rankled at every mention of it.

Now it was my turn to arch my pointed eyebrow at him.

Father continued. "I will enforce a truce while she does my bidding. No one may initiate an attack from either side while she is gone, or the offending party—soldiers, civilians, and gods—will face the wrath of the High King."

I didn't like the addition of civilians. Even Ares' people didn't deserve the same punishment as the demon standing beside me who started all of this.

Father's eyes slid to me. "You leave tomorrow."

I frowned. "I need to gather my armies—"

"Your army will stay in Eriset. The Beyond is wild and unorganized. Is the Queen of War incapable of taming such a land alone?"

This was ludicrous. He'd mentioned nothing about this to me.

Ares' posture relaxed into something insufferably smug. I snarled at him, unable to direct all my anger toward my father, who could grant Ares complete victory in one command if I defied him too openly.

I'd rather go to Abaddon.

Maybe this was... not the worst. I could stay longer, draw out the truce, have time to plan.

"I am capable," I replied, glancing at the gashes on Ares' arm that were already beginning to heal, though blood still dripped on the immaculate floor.

"I know you are, daughter. This is just what we need." Thenios beamed.

The prospect ahead exhausted me. With an army, I could rule in days. Without one, I'd have to be more careful. My reputation might be enough, but Urd wasn't one of the Realms. Did they know all the stories too?

Alone. In a fundamental way, I was always alone. How different could this be?

At least my people would have a better chance at safety with my father finally protecting them. My petitions had done nothing. The flayed corpses hadn't moved him. It was his own desire for more power that finally forced his hand.

"Agree with the terms of the truce," Thenios told Ares.

A command. Used for something good, for once.

Agree with the terms of the truce. My heart thundered. *The truce, the truce, the truce...*

Though Ares' eyes darkened, he obeyed.

The High King demanded my agreement next. This meant not only the temporary peace terms, but everything else we had discussed about my mission.

Alone, I would go to the Beyond, conquer it, and become its divine queen. Secretly, I'd scheme to win my own kingdom as well. Ares be damned.

This wasn't my twin's victory. It would be mine.

✿ *6* ✿

TYR

Maybe I was on the side of humans. The one underneath me felt so good.

She gasped and craned her neck, wrapping her legs tighter around me. She was so small that I had to remember to be careful. I couldn't release all my desire at once, though I still thrust hard. My instinct was to shove her down farther, bring her to the edge of danger, and pull her out again right as she orgasmed.

Even my fantasies were violent. All that pent-up confusion and frustration coming to the surface. I was too much and still somehow not enough.

"What do you want?" I panted. I'd be enough for this human girl. I'd make her forget any other lover as she lost herself in the little death.

Sweat coated her face and chest as she blearily focused on me. I took handfuls of her curves.

"What do you want me to do?" I demanded again.

The question seemed to take her aback. "Slow," she said, "and deep."

I plunged into her more slowly, against my roaring instincts demanding ferocious sex. She released a high moan. I repeated the motion, focusing on the way her slippery skin touched all the way up my shaft. It did feel good.

"Oh, Tyr!"

That was fast. Already, she contracted around me, belly trembling. I rolled my hips one more time before she fell apart.

I slid out, hard and aching. She watched as I made myself come. Not my favorite ending, but at least we were both satisfied to a degree.

She trailed a damp finger down the muscles of my chest. I gave a crooked smile and leaned closer.

"This is my favorite one," she said, pointing to a small T-shaped tattoo above my heart.

I had much larger designs covering most of my body. "Why that one?"

"My brother had a similar one before he died."

My body tensed. We had just met for a quick lay. Should I have known about her brother already? I chose my next question carefully. "How did he die?"

"Banewolf."

I exhaled. Not the gods, then.

But the heat between us was quickly dissipating.

"I'm sorry," I said, kissing her forehead and sitting up on my knees.

She eyed me with hungry appreciation. Did she know I had a Banewolf? She had to. I'd been performing my duties for fifty years. Fen had been with me for six. A Banewolf trotting alongside a god of battle wasn't exactly a common sight.

Here came the hard part. I'd chosen this girl as I did my nocturnal rounds because she seemed free spirited and downright sexy. But I couldn't bed her again. Relationships weren't an option for me. Especially with humans.

I'd defend the humans' basic rights. Occasionally, when my good sense failed, I'd fuck one of them. But they could never stay in my life.

Better to let her know now. Let her think me a heartless bastard. Most of Urd already thought so. Only my body, never aging, gave women a reason to look past that reputation.

"I have duties early in the morning," I said, standing and tugging on my clothes.

"I'll make you breakfast."

"I have to go."

"Wait." Now her voice had some of the disbelieving irritation I recognized.

"I have to go."

"I thought…"

"You thought I was different from the others. Sorry." I forced myself to meet her eyes. Anger had replaced lust.

At least she would just curse me and move on.

This probably wasn't what Hild was talking about when she encouraged me to find the women who wanted me. My gut clenched at the thought of her, with her veined fingers and cataracts in her eyes. We were so close. I still considered her my best friend. The pain of losing her loomed like an army on the horizon, ready to rip me apart.

I pursed my lips. I needed to stop doing this. It just

reminded me of the truth behind my monstrous reputation and left me more isolated than before.

I hadn't even learned this girl's name. Easier to let go that way.

I was a heartless bastard.

"Tyr."

"Gods and humans," I muttered, slinging Peacekeeper in its loop.

There was a small number of gods who fraternized with humans. Freya, for example, acted as though she couldn't stay away from them. She was an old god, though you wouldn't know it to look at her perfect body. Maybe that put her out of touch. I'd had to step between her and human antagonists more than once. Most, however, stayed scrupulously separate except on holidays newly appointed to honor us. The gods. Those ceremonies struck me as ludicrous, but not attending, they said, was an affront to the divine power. So I went.

The girl on the bed sighed. I had the power here, and she knew it.

"Night," I grunted.

As I left, I cursed myself. Fen, waiting outside the house, nudged my hand with his nose. I scratched his head. Next time, I should have someone stop me before I did something else that made me feel like shit.

THE NEXT MORNING, I WAS FUMING. BETWEEN ANGER AT myself for last night and anger at the other gods for thwarting my every attempt to reach some kind of justice in this godsforsaken place, I felt the rage radiating off me like heat. Everyone made way for me as I stalked through the Godlands on my rounds. Even the hair on Fen's ruff stood on end.

"Prisoner for you," said a soldier the moment I walked into the Great Hall, leaving Fen outside. Even some of the gods feared Banewolves. If they were too afraid to enter while he stood there, I wouldn't apologize.

I ground my teeth. One day, I'd have to delegate some of this work. If there was anybody I could trust to handle it.

"Who?"

"One of the leaders of the Human's Liberation."

"Which one?"

"Magnus Ivarssen."

We fell in step through the wooden hallways and descended a dark flight of stairs.

"What has he done now?"

"He was found inside Hrafnir's home."

I halted on the darkened stairway. "Inside his home? Why wasn't there an alert?" I snapped. King Hrafnir's house here in Urd wasn't as magnificent as his citadel in Varafjall in the north, but it was still the best place in town. Better than the Great Hall.

"He wasn't aggressive when we found him. He was…"

"What?" I had no patience at all.

"He was drunk. He'd been drinking the All-Father's stores."

"Stealing and trespassing," I said under my breath. "Why can't everyone just stay in their own fucking houses for once?"

We reached the landing. All the temporary holding cells were down here. Longer-term prisoners were housed farther away, in an actual prison. Down the dim passageway carved into the earth under the meeting house, there were rows of iron bars. As usual, a raucous commotion erupted at my arrival. Automatically, I reached for the ax handle. Once I reached the prisoner I needed to talk to, the others had better be quiet. I was in no mood to tolerate fools today. Someone could lose a finger, or worse.

"Anything else you need?" asked the soldier, eyeing me uncertainly.

Justice, justice, I chanted to myself. What did justice mean anymore?

"No," I growled. I knew Magnus Ivarssen. The soldier didn't need to show me.

I found his tawny beard and unruly hair immediately. He sat crouched in one of the first cells, still wavering from drink.

"Silence!" I roared. The din subsided to a murmur. Cocking my jaw, I glared at Magnus. "Hrafnir's house? Do you want a taste of Peacekeeper's blade?"

The man looked up at me, his light eyes piercing even in the gloom. He gave a sloppy smile. "Show'm gods," he slurred.

I narrowed my eyes. "You're only alive right now because I will it and because whoever caught you is incompetent. Now, what were you doing in that house?"

"I jus' want what's mine," he said, gesturing so fervently that he almost toppled to the side.

"Did anyone go with you?"

"I asked. They wouldn' come."

"*Who* wouldn't come?" I sensed the power in my limbs,

strength that could crush this dirty human at a whim. He had no godblood, so the Council wouldn't criticize me for doing it.

"You know," he drawled.

"The Liberation?" I guessed through gritted teeth.

He touched the tip of his nose. "They didn' wanna go."

"Probably because they have the basic instinct to survive."

The law had yet to be written down, but the understanding among gods and humans was that the punishment for a human entering a god's house uninvited meant death.

I was angry enough to do it. It would relieve some of the rage building inside me. But Magnus hadn't harmed anyone and he was too stupid to have tampered with Hrafnir's things. What were a couple jugs of mead to the most powerful god on the continent?

I didn't open the cell door separating us. I couldn't trust my mood.

"Lord Tyr!"

I whirled. Because of all the background noise, I hadn't heard the same soldier as before approaching again. After seeing his expression of urgency, I didn't relax my hold on the ax handle.

"What?"

"We need you. Right now."

"What's happening?" I demanded, gladly leaving the fool in his cell. Let him rot there.

I ran with the soldier back up the stairs.

"At the shore, it's..." But the soldier was out of breath.

"*What?*"

"They think it's Bellona, goddess of war."

❧ 7 ❧

BELLONA

Urd was too far away to travel through the air safely without sailing part of the way. But now I finally stood alone on the shore—a rocky beach, not even a port. Not knowing exactly where to materialize, I'd missed my aim by half a league and had to walk through pools and pines along the water's edge until I saw a sign of life. Humans bending over lobster traps and mending nets stopped to gawk at me. Their tanned skin and brown hair lightened by the sun made them seem untamed. They'd lived hard lives with few resources. I knew that savage look in their eyes.

When they saw me, many bowed low. At least they knew a goddess when they saw one, even if they didn't know my exact identity. Others, though, glared in disbelief, as if I'd offended them.

Maybe Thenios was right that this place was uncivilized.

Be diplomatic. Draw this out.

My lip curled in a sneer. Diplomatic. I made no promise to be discreet. I longed for peace, yes, but I longed for battle too.

The longer I stayed here, though, the more chance my subjects in Eriset had of resting from the constant violence. If I did this right, these people could help me cast out Ares for good.

"Where is your leader?" I asked. Hopefully they spoke my language. Foreign tongues weren't my gift. Casting someone away with a violent burst of air was. No need to use that now, though.

"You can talk to me." The deep voice had a heavy accent. I heard him before I saw who the voice belonged to.

A man as tall as I was, holding an ax in one closed fist. His brown hair was short, his bare chest covered in black designs. He was lithe, not bulky, but obviously strong. I took in his defined pectoral muscles, shoulders, biceps. Around his waist, strapped to his low-slung pants, hung other weapons. My gaze trailed back up again. Stubble on a hard-planed face. His ice-green eyes showed no submission, only anger.

At his side strode a gray wolf twice the size of any I'd witnessed before. It mirrored the man's predatory movements.

I held out a gauntleted hand. "Who are you?"

"Tyr, god of war."

I smirked. One of the new gods. I thought so. "There already is a god of war and it isn't you."

His jaw flexed as he marched closer, light dappling his sculpted body. His expression proclaimed loudly that he'd oppose me, but fuck me, he was gorgeous.

"Where is your leader?" I asked again.

"None of us are interested in entertaining a war goddess right now. We have enough problems without the Realms adding to them."

My eyebrows arched. Did he want to be ripped in half?

"We've never met," I said, poison dripping from the words, "so I'll assume your words are the result of idiocy. No one refuses a goddess, especially a goddess of war." I stepped very close to Tyr, within range of the ax. The wolf growled. It was a hot day, but I could have sworn I felt his body heat through my leather too. Carefully, I placed one sharp fingertip under his chin as I stared at him, eye to eye. "I haven't even said what I wanted."

He glared at me, stone-faced.

I lowered my voice to a menacing whisper. "It isn't to be entertained."

When I removed my fingernail from his chin, he exhaled. "What is it you want?" he asked, sullen.

"I know your land has problems. I can solve them."

His gaze swept over me. I could almost sense him counting the visible weapons I had with me and the armies I didn't. When he met my eyes again, he gave a dark smirk. "You don't know our problems here."

My blood woke up. I wanted to know. I wanted to battle the guilty.

I wanted to climb inside that voice and bathe in it.

I shook myself. This wasn't the time—or the god—for stupid fantasies.

The attention of the humans around us pierced my consciousness again. Something had shifted for them in the last part of our conversation. They were concerned. About what?

"I've already asked twice, so I won't ask again," I said. "Bring me to your leader so I can learn about these problems. Have the old gods come?"

The wolf growled softly beside us, enormous, but I knew

when men or animals would attack. Neither Tyr for all his bravado nor his pet would attack me.

To punctuate my command, I patted the creature's neck. It snarled but didn't strike. I looked pointedly at Tyr.

He couldn't hide his surprise at my gesture. After a pause, he slung his ax in a loop at his hip and turned. "Come on."

I didn't. No one called me like a fucking pet.

The ache in my chest rose to a roar. I didn't come on this damn mission to be disrespected. If diplomacy had been a person, I'd have struck it across the face.

He took a couple long strides away before he realized I hadn't followed. He gave me a sidelong glance.

"You never asked who I am," I said, mustering composure. My voice stayed low, but the snarl in my lip and crackling fury in our locked eyes gave me away.

"We all know who you are."

"Not well enough. Say my name."

His tattooed stomach rose and fell with a breath. "Bellona, goddess of war from the Eight Realms."

"Yes, Tyr, who will maybe be god of something someday. You're lucky to have your head. That should be enough of a gesture of peace for you."

"King Hrafnir rules here," he said after a pause. Words didn't have fangs anymore, though he was still clearly unhappy I'd arrived.

I'd heard that name. "Bring me."

Tyr waited until I reached him to keep walking. His wolf bristled, a lot like him. I matched them stride for stride.

With a deep breath, I composed myself. The truce with Ares was worth nothing if it didn't hold for a while. And there were problems that needed solving. Battles to be fought. Wrongdoers to be executed. I could bring swift order, once I understood the stakes.

Tyr and his dog had to move aside.

To reach the Great Hall we had to cross a huge rent in the earth. Thick boards created a ramp where the difference in height wasn't as pronounced. Ladders leaned against other places.

"Human side," Tyr grunted, gesturing to the lower ground. His mood hadn't improved on our walk. "Godlands." And he stalked up the ramp, his huge companion trotting next to him.

So humans and gods didn't get along. The picture started to come together. New gods against humans who were either jealous or oppressed by the more powerful, or both.

I sized up Tyr. I could see him earning those reactions easily. If I were a delicate human, I'd fear his ax and his wolf. I'd covet his strength and his body.

Urd was mostly forest, as far as I could see. Everything was underdeveloped, from the small wooden buildings to the lack of solid roads. Where trees grew near the crisscrossing paths, the base of the trunks were decorated with shining stones and little offerings. Reverence for the trees—was that why they didn't have roads? Not enough space to build without tearing them down? That was different.

Signs of war scored the land, but the threat didn't taste the same as it did on Eriset. This was aftermath that had never settled. Discontent that had brewed for years, an economy unable to recover, mobs or vigilantes doing stupid shit...

Not as many people as I would have guessed. Lots of heat and quiet. The ambush sounds of footsteps and wind. I flexed my gauntlet.

Nothing seemed grand enough for a "Great Hall." Yet Tyr stopped at a low wooden building—smaller than a palace, smelling slightly of rot—and ordered the dog to sit by the door.

The inside was a little better. Still rot-smelling. The ceiling in the large oval room seemed higher than it looked outside. At one end, a carved throne sat elevated above the rest. It had handles or perches off the sides and a green cushion on the seat. Hrafnir's, but he didn't sit on it.

Nobody was here. Why was everything so empty? Even after mass casualties, Eriset still teemed like an anthill.

More unsettling was the lack of exits. No windows. Two exterior doors. A hallway that might lead to a third.

A bearded young man appeared in the hallway. His gray tunic and lack of weapons didn't suggest a warrior. His height made me think he was deathless, though.

"Where's Hrafnir?" Tyr demanded.

The man squeaked and fell to one knee, eyes perfectly round before he dropped them to the floor.

"Answer," I said.

"At home."

"Shit," Tyr hissed. "Why?"

"A member of Human's—"

"What did Magnus do?"

"The king is checking his belongings."

Tyr's eyes darted, mouth twisting in a half-snarl. Finally, he turned to me. "He's unavailable."

"Not if I demand to talk."

"Your majesty..." He hadn't used that title before. It sounded good coming out of that mouth. Much better than *come on.* "Someone broke into the king's house this morning. He's setting things in order." He clamped his teeth down. "Would you wait?" His features softened a little, muscles unclenching. "You said you're here for peace."

Here for peace. "Yes," I bit out.

His eyebrows said the retort he held back. *So they sent the goddess of war?* Wisely, he didn't say it aloud.

TYR

This wasn't good. If Hrafnir returned and something had been stolen or destroyed—*the liquor was stolen,* I reminded myself—then he would hate that I hadn't executed Magnus already. My inaction would confirm the gods' slanders that I was on the side of the humans.

It wasn't my fault that the goddess of war had appeared on our shores minutes after I'd been sent to deal with the criminal.

Now, she stood, metal-tipped fingers trailing over various knives tucked into her tight leather outfit. The clothes looked tough and functional, ideal for movement without extraneous fabric in the way. When we met, she had eyed my bare chest as if it were a point of weakness for her claws to pierce. I almost felt that way myself while she glared through fierce eyes masked in a thick stripe of black warpaint. Leather would be heavy for our hot season, though.

If she stayed.

She couldn't. I'd find some way to make this new threat

leave. Her attitude suggested she had never lost a battle or an argument, but I'd find some way to send her off. Bellona had to be here for conquest, not peace.

Look at her.

Everything she was and did declared war. None of the women, even the goddesses, in Urd were as muscular as she was. The sides of her head had been shaved almost to the scalp, leaving dark, braided hair running down the center. She bristled with violence, simmered with it. She was almost like a Banewolf that way. Ferocious and striking.

She cut a glance at me. "How much longer?"

"I don't know." Our inaction grated on me too, but I couldn't leave her alone in the Great Hall. She seemed volatile enough to attack everyone here. The Council of the Gods wasn't in session, but servants cleaned the inner rooms this time of day. The longer we waited, the more likely an attack seemed.

"What do you know?" she snapped. "What power do you have here?"

A grim half-smile crossed my lips. "I keep the peace."

She squared herself at me. Remarkably tall. "Then what is preventing peace?" She said it slowly, as though I were dumb-witted.

You. "Every nation has conflict. Doesn't yours?"

A small blade flew into her fist. The angle of our bodies prevented the servant from seeing it.

I'd been stabbed before. The pain didn't change, even though I was a god, only the healing.

Her voice lowered to a whisper. "I tire of you and your disrespect. It's no wonder your land is dangerous and backward, with you as law." She tapped her knife blade against my exposed stomach, a smile more horrifying than her grimace melting over her features. She enjoyed menacing me, teasing the skin she could easily flay open. She let the tip catch on a ridge of a muscle before scraping harmlessly away.

"Dangerous and backward?" I echoed. Who did this woman think she was? I was a god, not a human to be talked down to and intimidated. "I'm sure King Hrafnir will appreciate your input." Maybe that was the way to get rid of her. It would take no effort at all to make her expose her true motivations—battle and conquest, blood and resources. Hrafnir would see and banish her back to her own lands. Even the goddess of war was only one being, while we were many.

She sheathed the weapon in one flawless motion. It made me want to test the technique on Peacekeeper.

"I'm going to find him," she announced.

"He won't be pleased. And he's a god-king." I leveled a glare at her but she merely stalked away.

"I'm a god-queen," she replied. "And I defended my lands hundreds of years before your little king was born."

"Peace?" I reminded her, jogging to keep up. She was like a rainstorm, destructive and inevitable. I hated feeling one step behind. As though that hadn't been my entire existence. I never stood as steadily on my own two feet as I wanted to.

"You'll have it when you meet my demands." She didn't even look at me.

"Stop." I grabbed her arm as we reached the main door.

Her knife flew out again. Heat bit the tops of my fingers. When I looked down, they were bleeding. The slash that cut them wasn't very deep, but my hand dripped with blood.

She hadn't missed. It was a message. *Don't touch me.*

I didn't back down. Crowding her space, I got close to her as she'd done to me.

Bellona was a force, but so was I. My entire life had been struggle and I wasn't about to let this one goddess ruin any chance of peace for Urd. Despite her protests, I didn't believe a word. She'd barely arrived and she'd threatened me multiple times.

"You are one goddess," I growled. "You may be older than the earth but we still outnumber you. Tread more carefully." I separated each word.

She still gripped the knife but I didn't fucking care anymore. Raising my bloodied hand, I wiped off the fingers on her bare shoulder. With a narrow gaze to punctuate the gesture, I straightened.

Was I imagining it, or did the slightest flush darken her neck? Her pupils looked a little larger too.

I allowed the smirk on my face. Bellona wasn't made of iron. She was flesh and blood too, and something I'd done had turned her on.

She saw my realization at the same time and grew even angrier. My smug look faded an instant before a powerful gust of air shot me backward into the nearest wall. Muttered words carried on the wind, "Fuck you."

Before I could right myself, Bellona had disappeared.

I stepped through the air in the direction Tyr's eyes had wandered every time he mentioned Hrafnir. I didn't know exactly where this northern god's house was, but I sure as fuck knew I didn't want to wait around in the dirty meeting hall anymore.

I'd lost my temper, struck out at Tyr, but he'd deserved it for grating on my last godsdamned nerve. I don't think I'd ever found my temper, to be honest.

This place was suffocating. Could I even stall long enough to give my people a reprieve? I was a creature of blood and battle. As evident by my arrival, I couldn't hold back for long. My instincts roared to conquer, conquer, conquer. Not play nice.

Thenios was a fool to send me.

"Hrafnir," I bit out as I materialized in front of a couple wide-eyed women. New goddesses, from the height of them. "Where is he?"

I still held the bloody knife in my fist, I realized.

Yeah, Thenios was an absolute, fucking fool.

"I don't know," one of them stammered.

"His house. Where is it? Where does he live?"

The other women, frowning with concentration as if trying to remember where she'd heard of me, pointed northward through the trees.

Without a word, I left them, marching toward the house. I had to calm myself or I'd eviscerate someone. My chest ached. I didn't expect to hate this assignment as much as I already did. My castle in Eriset sounded like a haven compared to this place. There, I had my generals. I had respect. My people knew I'd protect them unless they crossed me. The perfect balance. Here, it was chaos, and not the fun kind.

I forced myself to wipe off my knife and sheathe it. Tyr's blood still oozed down my shoulder, I realized. I brushed it off, but my heart beat harder at the thought of his eyes, so full of rage, and the absolutely ballsy choice to smear me with the blood I'd shed from him. I bet his hands would fit around my throat. I exhaled a long breath.

A wooden building came in sight through the trees. Nothing lay around it. It almost could have been abandoned. The style was very similar to the meeting house, nicer, but without the well-worn path to the door. Two stories. Golden accents.

I stalked up the deer trail to the door.

"Hrafnir!"

No one appeared.

I called out again, opening the gold-crusted door to peer inside. I fought the urge to handle one of my weapons again, just in case. They were old friends to me. But I resisted.

Damn it, where was this supposed king? No wonder this place was in shambles. Between the alleged peacekeeper and the absentee king, this place had no chance of order.

"King Hrafnir!"

A bird in a nearby tree squawked and flew away. That was it. If he didn't respond, I would return to the meeting place and set up my reign there. He could suck a dick for all I cared.

Finally, a thickly bearded man appeared in dark blue robes. He had one eye, but it was piercing and alive enough for two. How had he lost it? Things like that were possible, but extraordinarily rare. Even I had just a couple scars. The rest had knitted over.

Hrafnir. One of the older gods of the north. I'd been mildly curious to meet him, though I hadn't realized it until right now.

"Why do you come here?" he asked in a measured voice, although the wariness in his gaze was enough to tell me that he knew who I was.

I'd give him this. He had courage.

"To offer my protection. To set your land in order." I couldn't keep all the derision from my tone. This place was a sty.

"Protection." The word had no inflection at all, but I could tell there were several questions lurking under it.

I stepped back from the doorway to let in more light, gesturing outward. "Talk with me." *Yes, conversation, my greatest strength.*

His jaw flexed. Maybe he was wondering why Tyr hadn't stopped me from getting this far. Speaking of him, where was he? Surely he'd guessed where I was by now.

"You are Bellona, goddess of war. And you want to talk?" His eye grazed the knife hilts flush against my body.

"Would the"—I sucked in a slow breath—"meeting place make you more comfortable to talk about a deal that would benefit both of us?"

"More should be in audience," he agreed.

Impatience roared up in me again, but I stuffed it down with a practiced hand. I inclined my head in a nod and stepped back into that squeezing gap in space back to the meeting hall. Much faster than walking, now that I knew the way.

This time, I was alone. No sign of Tyr.

No sign of Hrafnir.

I waited a few beats longer. Was the king not coming? My face flushed hot with frustration. This felt like dealing with children.

I stepped back through the air to Hrafnir's residence. From there, I could see him walking back, as though he felt no urgency at all.

As I caught up to him, I spied Tyr running from the opposite direction, the wolfdog at his side. He looked somewhat surprised to see me. Did he think I'd just vanish, give up the fight? Or... diplomacy?

I cursed myself. I wasn't cut out for this.

The three of us met under the trees.

"Was my summons not clear?" I said to Hrafnir, injecting as much sweetness as I could into the question.

Tyr's eyebrows popped up. Whether he was surprised by my changed tone or the words themselves, directed at his king, I couldn't tell. "No one orders the king," he said.

Hrafnir gave Tyr a look that silenced him.

Interesting.

"I agreed to convene," Hrafnir said.

Then why are you walking so godsdamn slowly?

"Do you need time to... think?" I guessed, falling in step with the two of them.

Hrafnir ignored me.

Ignored me.

My throat constricted.

"My prized hunting trophy is gone," he told Tyr. "I hope you finished him."

"I was pulled away before—"

Hrafnir stopped walking. Gods, this was taking forever. "You didn't execute Magnus?"

"I had to attend to Bellona. An emissary from the Eight Realms doesn't arrive every day. I was in the middle of asking him questions."

Hrafnir scoffed. "Questions."

Tyr's eyes darkened. "Yes, questions." After a beat of hesitation, he added, "My king. I want to find out the truth before I execute someone."

"He broke into my house." Hrafnir's voice thundered. He seemed more like a god than he had before.

The only evidence that Tyr was affected by the king's threatening tone was a slight tightening of muscle. "He's an idiot, but I didn't know he'd stolen—"

"Is that not enough? Breaking into my home? The home of the *king of the gods*?"

Tyr set his mouth in a resolute line.

"I'll kill him for you," I interjected.

The other two stared at me. I looked levelly back.

This was actually a good solution. If I killed this Magnus person, I'd gain Hrafnir's trust, put myself in good standing above his current keeper of the peace, and get out some of the violence that itched beneath my skin.

My eyes fell to Tyr's hand, which still bled.

"No," Tyr said.

I drew myself up, the ghost of a smile on my face. "Do you think he's innocent, then?" I asked. "Hrafnir was threatened."

"If he's guilty, then I'll do it," Tyr insisted.

I turned a self-satisfied smile toward the king. Let him decide. He would choose me for the job. No one liked an insurrectionist.

"I'm here to help you," I nudged. "Let me prove it. Show me where he is."

Hrafnir turned his blazing eye from me to Tyr and back. "Very well."

The wolfdog growled, probably sensing his master's mood. I met Tyr's furious gaze. My gut clenched. He was beautiful when he was angry.

Maybe I could manage to salvage this trip after all.

BELLONA

Now, I suspected we walked so that Tyr's rage could cool down. It didn't. I would have preferred to travel by stepping through the air, but neither of them made a move toward that option.

Magnus, the one who'd broken into Hrafnir's home, was apparently back in the Great Hall. I could have dealt with this even sooner.

When it finally came in sight, I was itching to see him, to watch the terror grow on his face as he realized the queen of war had come for him. This was a role I could relish. I wasn't built for peace.

My mind flitted briefly back to my home country. Ares—curse him—had better be holding up his end of the imposed truce, or this all would have been for nothing. I could just see him taking his army somewhere he could deny responsibility, claiming a rogue group had killed key leaders in my company. The idea set my blood burning.

Regaining my focus, I spotted the meeting house through

the trees. Finally. My fingers itched for my knife.

Tyr had stopped bleeding, but his hand was still stained. Why hadn't either he or the king mentioned it? Were wounds so common?

Tyr's wolf remained outside as we entered. My steps grew eager as the king remained behind and Tyr led me to a staircase off the hall. I knew better than to descend in front of him, exposing myself to the risk of a surprise attack, so I gestured for him to lead the way.

Which weapon to choose? I selected a long blade, hardy but thin.

At the bottom of the steps lay a row of stinking cells. Tyr seethed as he marched forward. I watched his tattooed back with appreciation now. At least now I knew better where I stood. And it was above him.

His muscular shoulders rose in obvious frustration. My eyes roved down to the divot at the base of his spine, where tattoos disappeared under his low-slung pants.

"Here," he grunted at the end of the short passage. He turned around and crossed his arms over his generous chest.

I felt more expansive now. Happier. If he had wanted to fuck me right here, I would have let him.

I followed his gaze to the cell on the right, where a human man crouched, his bleary eyes as wide as circles. I smiled, feline. "Magnus?" I asked.

In a blink, I stood inside the cell. No need to open the door. Even that small jump felt good after so much slow walking to get here.

Magnus recoiled.

I sensed Tyr's anger behind me, his jaw set hard enough to

crack teeth. Let him seethe. Just because he wouldn't choose a more violent form of justice didn't mean he needed to begrudge me the satisfaction.

Magnus didn't have time to scream. In a heartbeat, I'd cut his head clean off. Blood sprayed up on my leather outfit as the body slumped to the floor.

I sighed. I knew the expression I wore behind my black streak of warpaint was feral. I met Tyr's gaze briefly before I stepped through the air to the upper level where Hrafnir waited to meet with me.

Fuck me. She was crazy.

The look Bellona gave me after decapitating Magnus, whose corpse still glugged out blood, was an animal over its kill. This excited her.

And, if I was honest with myself, it excited me a little too. She didn't hesitate. If there was a terrible thing to be done, she didn't censor herself or overthink the assignment. She was probably more capable than anyone else I'd met. If she weren't so unpredictable and threatening, she could actually be useful in this fight for a more just society.

But she was unpredictable and threatening. She didn't know Magnus, didn't know his level of guilt, yet here she was stealing any honor I could have gained by executing him myself. My mind snagged at that idea. I probably wouldn't have. For violent offenders, people who could hurt themselves or others by their actions, I had little mercy. For idiots like this, I had contempt but no bloodlust. The other gods couldn't understand why I distinguished between the humans that way. Why not kill more of them?

Because I didn't want us to become monsters.

Too late for that.

I left behind Magnus' lifeless body and staring head to trudge upstairs. Bellona had disappeared between one heartbeat and the next. I'd heard of abilities like that, but the ramifications of a goddess like Bellona having the ability to appear anywhere at will chilled my blood. I'd never witnessed the skill myself. Was it something all gods were supposed to be able to do? If so, Hrafnir had never showed us.

I set my teeth together. He hadn't shown us a lot of things.

There was a strict hierarchy in Urd and it went old gods, young gods, humans. Old gods didn't think much of us. I was excited when they first came, expecting them to help me fit into this new body, show me what it meant to be deathless. I'd respected—no, worshipped—these gods before I became one. But now I suspected Hrafnir was more interested in establishing dominance than actually helping us with anything.

I topped the stairs, turned. Several more gods and goddesses than had been present this morning filed in and took their places in the main room. Hrafnir sat on his throne. Bellona didn't sit at all. She stood in the place I had earlier, one hand on her hip. She'd sheathed the knife she used to kill the prisoner, but the entire room still smelled like blood. I snuffed the scent out of my nose. It didn't seem to bother her at all. No surprise. She was a maniac.

Hrafnir observed my entrance. I said nothing. What was there to say? In just a few hours, this visitor from the Eight Realms had found favor with the king by doing something I disagreed with. If Bellona earned more power, it could only mean destruction for the human towns.

Hild's face flashed before my mind and I tried to calm myself. I'd be damned before Bellona laid a single finger on my friend.

"Bellona, Queen of War, goddess from the Eight Realms, you wanted to talk," King Hrafnir began.

I almost laughed. Moments ago she'd executed a stranger. Talking wasn't what she was best at.

"After executing the human who trespassed in my home, you've earned the right to speak."

My budding smile turned back to a scowl.

"Thenios wishes to make you a Ninth Realm in exchange for our protection. I would oversee."

The rest of the people in audience gasped or whispered or froze in horror. There. I knew she wouldn't be delicate. I couldn't stop one side of my lips from lifting.

As if she could see behind her, she shot me a glare. Speckles of blood coated her face like freckles.

I sauntered to my customary seat, close to the king. This would be good.

"We have no wish to be part of the Eight Realms," the king answered. He seemed more comfortable now that he was surrounded by others who would protect him if she chose to attack.

She can cross space in a moment. The thought made me finger the shaft of Peacekeeper.

"It's an honor," she said, her voice and posture both hard as iron.

"Thank you," said King Hrafnir, "but we have no need of your... protection."

Bellona released a breath from her nose. "That's the kind version of the offer. I suggest you take it. Little will change under my rule except that you will experience more order than you're used to, and you'll have a more competent queen."

Hrafnir paused as though unsure what to say. I closed my hand around the ax handle.

"Go back to your lands, Queen Bellona," he said gently. "For your service, I thank you, but we have no need of you here."

"I think you do. This place is a shithole."

Gasps from the audience.

"And the gods are so new they don't know what to do with their powers. I have experienced more of life than everyone here put together. Let me put your land in order. I'd hate to burn it."

The room went utterly silent. Bellona met my eyes again, this time with a request in addition to a breath of challenge. A request for what? Support?

My insides writhed at the implication of her words. Submit or die. Goddesses couldn't be permanently killed or else I'd devise that way to get us out of this situation. Hrafnir's bald refusal wasn't getting us anywhere either. Maybe there was a deal we could strike that could satisfy all parties and leave no one dead.

I stood, releasing my hold on the ax.

Hrafnir's eye widened but he inclined his head to let me speak. Surprising, after the debacle with Magnus.

"Goddess," I began, "please give us time to consider."

"What is there to consider?"

Her brusque manner grated on me. She had a home. Why did she need mine except to satisfy her bloodlust and greed? I steadied myself. "These changes would be monumental. There's much to consider. You can't expect all of Urd to make up their minds instantly."

She cast me an almost amused look, as though they absolutely could, when faced with her.

"Well said."

My attention shot to the king seated beside me. His comment was brief, unremarkable, but I knew it for what it was—forgiveness for my earlier blunder. Part relieved and part annoyed, I nodded at him and sat.

"Would you consent to a week?" the king asked Bellona.

She stood, uncharacteristically unsure. Finally, after scanning the assembled gods, she said, "I accept those terms. A week to decide."

My clenched muscles relaxed. She wouldn't lash out today, at any rate. I could figure out some way to protect my king and my best friend from this force of nature.

"Our eternal gratitude," the king replied mildly. "Until then, you will stay with Tyr."

My jaw dropped, protests crowding each other to escape my mouth.

"What?" she snapped.

"We have little space to accommodate someone of your stature, so the least we can give is hospitality," said the king.

I felt the real reasons for this decree radiating off him. *Keep her out of trouble.*

But she *was* trouble.

This was a punishment too, I felt sure. I hesitated to kill Magnus. I defended humans right before this. She, on the other hand, had felt no pity at all for their shorter, harder lives. She'd enjoyed killing Magnus. I saw it on her face. Was the king hoping I'd pick up more ruthlessness from her?

I had plenty as it was. I didn't want more.

Bellona appeared to see the humor in his statement too. Hospitality? Unless you somehow talked to Fen or Hild, you'd see I didn't extend hospitality to anyone. I did my job and went home. Which was pretty small. Not great for a famous goddess.

"I'll sleep here," she countered.

Wait? The Great Hall?

"She can stay with me."

I looked around for the speaker before I realized I had said the words. Like a fucking idiot. If Bellona slept here, she'd already taken over. I couldn't let that happen. Somehow, we had to get rid of her. Before my brain could form a logical thought, my mouth had stepped in with the first solution it had to stop her.

Too bad my mouth was so stupid.

Bellona looked as shocked as I felt.

"Perfect. In a week, we will reconvene," said Hrafnir with obvious relief. A few began to stir in the audience. "In the meantime, our honored guest will stay with you."

BELLONA

"I'll sleep outside."

Tyr reached toward me and wisely reconsidered. My shoulder was still smeared with the remnants of his blood from when I'd sliced a line down the top of his fingers the last time he tried to grab me.

"Don't do that," he ground out, as though the words pained him.

We stood just outside the meeting hall. The wolfdog had joined him, sitting at his side, taller than some of the humans I'd seen at the river. It looked perfectly content, unlike its owner.

The buzz of the kill wore off after Hrafnir's decree that I stay with Tyr. He was the person I'd spent the most time with today, but we'd seen enough of each other to know it wasn't a good idea to sleep under the same roof. Pain—for him, most likely—was sure to follow. I didn't know if I could control myself. He had no respect.

"I'll do as I please," I said.

His nose flared. "You agreed to let us have a week to mull over your... offer."

And you'd pretty damn well take it.

Truth be told, I would have agreed to a month, since that meant more time for my side of Eriset to breathe. To sleep without fear of violence. But I couldn't let Hrafnir know that, at least not yet.

Thank the gods I hadn't agreed to a month. If I had to spend all that time in the presence of this upstart, I'd go mad.

Or murderous.

Definitely murderous.

But I'd endured torture for longer than a week on numerous occasions. This couldn't be any worse than that. I'd ignore him. He'd go off and pretend to keep the peace some-times, and I'd be left alone.

"Where is it, then? Your house."

He steadied himself, unmoving, for a beat, never breaking eye contact, before he pivoted on the road. "This way," he muttered. His pet rose too and followed.

The sun was sinking, streaming blood red and rotten orange light.

Better than torture.

As I followed him, I reminded myself that I liked the view, even if I didn't like the attitude or obvious incompetence. Normally, I'd lead or at least walk abreast, but, if we walked side by side, he might have the foolish urge to talk. I preferred silence. And his ass.

His residence stood close to the fault line, the dividing line between the communities of gods and humans. At least that was the right place for him, given the situation here. A commander on the front lines. I mentally allotted half a point in his favor.

"This," he said, flicking his non-bloody hand lazily toward the little shelter. Some of the poorest in Eriset lived in houses like these, and Tyr was a god. It was a much smaller version of the house Hrafnir claimed, wooden, tucked in among the trees like a hunting cabin. Only one story with no stone or iron defenses. It was laughable. A single being with the power of flame could destroy everything he owned in seconds.

The only interesting feature were the ash trees that wove over the top as though their branches could protect him. For a second, the sight saddened me.

He opened the door and the wolfdog squeezed through the door. I hadn't seen it go into a building. It looked even bigger indoors, with teeth the size of my thumb. Half the main room was all muscle and gray fur.

Damn. I liked this creature.

When I glanced around, there wasn't much to see—a green and brown patterned rug under a thick wooden table, a deep armchair worn to the stuffing, and a sewn patch about the size of my hand clumsily tacked to the wall above an opening that led to other rooms. It showed a crossed ax and branch against a forest green background.

Tyr's scowl deepened to comical levels as he watched me survey the room.

Maybe this could almost be fun.

"Magnificent quarters," I remarked. "I'll just sleep in the corner. Or do you mind if I sleep in the chair?"

The words seemed to send him over the edge. "I didn't

invite you here, but I'm obeying the king. I don't trust you in my house—"

"This is a house?"

"—or in my country. I don't believe for a second that you're here for peace, Bellona, and if you touch anyone I care about, I'll show you war."

I hadn't expected such an outburst so quickly. In his deep, accented voice, the threat sounded delicious. This wasn't the inane opposition I feared, but a small, lovely fight. I'd play.

"You care about someone?"

He sneered, as if telling himself off for saying too much. "All of Urd."

"No, someone in particular. Beyond your dog."

The wolf's tongue lolled as it sat watching us. Its backside took up half the far wall.

"I have an extra bed down there," he said, pointing to the opening underneath the patch.

"For the person you care about?"

I could practically see steam coming from his rippling, tattooed skin. What would it feel like under my fingers...?

"You know what?" he said, whirling on me. "While you're in my house, I want you to relinquish all your weapons."

I laughed. Actually laughed.

"This is as hospitable as I can be. I don't trust you, but I'll let you stay here, so no weapons."

"You're serious?" My gaze flashed down to the blades hanging from his belt. "What about you?"

After a beat, he said, "I'll give up mine too, while we're inside."

I didn't point out how easy it would be to retrieve one in the middle of the night, if the need arose.

"All right, then," I said, a challenge in my tone, laughter still dying on my lips. "You first."

He pulled the ax from its loop at his waist and laid it pointedly on the table. Risky. Maybe brave but more likely naïve.

I moved to the opposite side of the table and took out the trusty knife I'd slashed his fingers with earlier, laying it beside the ax.

With snake-like speed, Tyr unsheathed a thick knife from his hip, brandishing it before setting it down.

Showing off, are we? I chose the decapitating knife next, circling it lazily through the air before putting it with the others.

Another stubby knife emerged from his pocket. He flung it expertly into the wood of the table between two other weapons.

I slid two knives out of their hiding places at once, copying his move, except that my blades formed an X against his.

It didn't look like he had anymore, but he undid his knotted belt without looking down, wrapping the rope firmly around one fist before releasing it in a coil.

His hands could definitely squeeze my throat. I felt my pulse between my legs as I drew out a thin vial from between my breasts. Poison. I opened both palms as though this were the beginning of a magic trick.

I waited. He didn't have anything else.

I continued to pull out a razor, a cord, a mirror, and two more knives. Tyr couldn't hide his expression of surprise—and maybe a little awe—as I kept finding pockets in my tight clothes to draw from. Finally, off came my metal tipped gloves.

When I stepped back from the table, it bristled with blades. A thousand ways to die.

The process had taken so long that the wolf had wandered outside for a piss. The room held just the two of us now.

"And?" he prompted.

"That's all."

Tyr approached my side of the table, his trousers riding even lower without the belt. Still, the tattoos reached lower, lower...

He raised his hand in a non-threatening gesture I knew better than to trust. Reaching up, he slid one more small blade from within my braids. "Then what's this?" He brandished it in front of my face, nearly touching my nose.

The slide against my skull, the challenge in the movement, the rasp in his voice that sounded like sex...

"Insurance," I purred. My heart beat heavily, familiar need pressing in. I plucked the knife from his fingers and flicked it into the table.

No harm in fucking the enemy, right? Tyr wasn't even the enemy. He was an aggravating roadblock. And right now he was a beautiful tower of tattooed muscle that wanted to get back at me for demanding his city. Sounded like a good time to me.

His green eyes blazed as he looked at me, from anger, lust —I didn't really care. I hooked two fingers into his waistband.

"What are you doing?" he snapped, grabbing my wrist and forcing me to let go, but not before I saw the bulge there get thicker.

"Maybe I'm playing with my prey," I said, using my other hand now.

He grabbed that one too, a tiny wince crossing his features. That was the hand I'd cut. Even so, his grip was strong. Long, forceful, calloused fingers. "I'm not prey." His voice dipped even lower, and so did his eyes.

"Prove it, then." I got wetter the longer he held me bound like that. Our gazes clashed as surely as the weapons.

He took deep, shaky breaths, glaring at me. I opened my mouth, inviting.

I saw the moment he decided.

"Fuck," he murmured, crashing his mouth into mine and hurling us both against the wall. My stomach flipped as he pressed the length of his body against me. Even through my clothes, his muscles flexed and contracted, drawing out a moan. He hadn't released my hands. He held both in one hand by the wrists above my head as he ground against me. He was hard. Really hard.

"Are you angry at me, huh?" I taunted, breathless already. "Show me. Show me how angry you are."

He growled and smashed my wrists into the wall above me. It barely hurt. With a sinuous roll of his body, he thrust against me, awakening my core. I didn't want him spread over me like this. I wanted us both to be naked, his cock plunged so deep inside me it felt like a knife thrust.

"That's nothing," I said. "Take me, if you want it."

His mouth never left mine except when I ripped away to talk. His lips, his tongue, found mine again in an angry conversation of lust. He kicked the door closed.

Good. I needed release. Gods, after the week I'd had, I needed a better release than I'd had in years.

He ground against me urgently. My breathing came more labored and I arched into him, trying to find that spot, that action that would make me wetter, find me that release.

I twisted one hand out of his grasp and reached again for the waistband, this time diving straight in. I found his cock warm and hard and waiting.

Wrapping my fingers around it, I wished for my gauntlet. "What... shall I do to you?" I panted.

"No," he snarled, jutting his palm against my chin, forcing my face upward. "What will I do to you?"

I smiled. "Squeeze."

✤ 13 ✤

TYR

I hadn't planned to fuck the goddess of war. But if that was what she wanted...

If it hadn't been for her infuriating face and her infuriating body and her infuriating poise. Fuck me, but as she pulled weapons from every conceivable crevice of her body, I found myself getting hard and dumb.

I was harder and dumber now. I knew this was a stupid thing to do even as I rolled my hips against her, crushing her fingers which were down my pants. *Oh gods.*

She said squeeze. Gladly. Bellona had chipped away at my reputation in front of the king and was threatening my nation. I'd squeeze her throat until she blacked out if that was what she wanted.

My fingers tightened around her throat. Her hand at my cock trembled.

Actually trembled.

She wasn't afraid. That emotion didn't exist in her. It was... arousal. My breath came out in heavy pants, gusting into her mouth as I bit down on her lip. Little by little, I tightened my fist.

She whimpered. The sound intoxicated me. I had to get inside her. Every grain of common sense could go to hell. In my excitement, I shook her. Her eyes rolled back in ecstasy. Had I ever met someone who liked it this rough before? Well, I could be rougher.

"Come on," I commanded, still gripping her by the throat. The movement released her hold on my erection, which throbbed for contact again. I wouldn't fuck on the floor like a dog.

Not this time.

I mentally shook myself, but couldn't come out of my lustful haze enough to figure out why that thought was wrong.

She was bigger than any other woman—or goddess—I'd been with, but she let me pull her down the hall to my room, to my bed, where I laid her down and climbed on top of her. There was so much of her, all leather and muscle and defiance. I could hardly see beyond the ache in my cock, the demand to get inside. I let her go long enough to strip off my pants. Her gaze lingered down there, tracing tattooed designs that ended right where my shaft began. The appreciation of a goddess like Bellona was as heady as any drunken night. She was a being who took what she wanted.

And right now, she wanted me.

I offered a feral smile. The crisscrossed leather top she wore came off in one piece. Her shoes and leather trousers next. She was danger personified, hard muscle and heavy breasts.

Even in my wanton, aching stupor, a tiny voice said that

she couldn't want the kind of ferocious sex I craved. If she hated it, she could visit vengeance on everyone in Urd.

But gods, if I didn't want to slap her and choke her and bury myself in her...

I settled over her again, gripping my cock in a fist. When I nudged against her, her pussy was hot and dripping.

Gods...

"No," she croaked.

I blinked, looked up.

"*Fuck* me, or don't do it at all."

My heart thundered so loud it drowned out my ragged breathing.

"Choke me. *Fuck me.* Can you do that? Or are you too much of a coward?"

Gods above. Bellona would drive me mad. My last thread of restraint snapped under those words. I hauled her forward, spreading her legs wide. Her hips were flexible. Very flexible. I hooked my hands beneath her thighs and dragged our bodies together, pushing my hard cock into her. I plunged in deep and hard once, twice.

"You can do better." Her eyes, hooded even through the black makeup, dared me to try more.

With a roar, I grabbed her throat again, more fiercely this time, feeling her pounding heartbeat in time with my thrusts. Her mouth opened in a grimacing smile, showing her canines.

She liked this? I could do this.

I stabbed into her, deep, deep, and cut off all her air. Her eyes closed. I did it again, not releasing her. She didn't fight.

Again.

"Fuck," I grunted, leaning into her. When I pulled partially out, I let her take a breath. She gasped out a laugh.

She was crazy.

And... fuck me... I liked it.

"More?" My own voice was so hoarse it sounded foreign in my ears.

Her sharply tipped breasts heaved. "More."

I pinched one of her nipples hard before giving her a slap.

"Afraid of hurting me?" she goaded.

I did the same thing to the other breast, but harder, ruthless. Human women would cry out in pain, demand that I stop, if I ever did this to them.

Bellona just put on a look of feline satisfaction, pinning me with a gaze so sensual, I thought I'd moan from that look alone.

With renewed rigor, I pounded into her, taking a rough handful of her hair and forcing her head back into the blankets. I choked her with the other hand. That seemed to be her favorite thing. Her skin flushed. Her mouth opened in a sinful groan.

I felt my release coming as she contracted around me.

Letting go of her hair, I slapped her across the face.

"Yes!" she lisped. Speaking was difficult around my squeezing fingers.

I hit her again. I never thought I'd meet someone who liked this. But the power it gave me... it was pure sex.

"Come for me," I demanded, my own orgasm shooting down my back, ready to explode out of me.

Not yet.

"Come for me!" The command this time was savage, a snarl. I dug my short nails into her full breast.

She resisted. I could feel her start to tremble, to squeeze my cock with her inner muscles, her quiet noises getting higher pitched. But she met my gaze with a look that said, "Make me."

Okay. I'd make her.

I sat up a little, making room for one hand to rub her center. Her eyes lit up.

My thrusts became jagged.

Any moment now.

But I didn't want to break first. Feeling reckless, I squeezed one finger alongside my pulsing dick and shoved it inside her. She gasped and arched. When I pulled it out, wet and slippery, I slapped her blood-stained cheek hard. She croaked out a strangled scream, and I pulled out in time to watch my heavy orgasm, hot and intense, shoot across her firm body.

Shaking, I came back into my right mind.

Bellona, goddess of war, lay spread across my blankets. Bellona, who wanted to conquer my country, who'd cut a man's head off, who was staying at my house for the next week, had demanded that I fuck her. Looking at her sweaty, red skin and disheveled hair, I knew I'd obeyed to her satisfaction.

And I got the sense that she would have liked it even rougher.

I drew a hand down my face, only realizing afterward that my palm had some of her black warpaint on it. The smart side of my brain told me I'd been an idiot, but the other side wanted to see how much she'd let me do next time.

The last flake of wood curled up at the point of my knife. My symbol of a torch for the life I'd taken yesterday. My flames meant bloodshed, meant conquest. They were a warning to my enemies to beware.

Thenios' phallic lightning bolt or Ares' spear was vain decoration by comparison.

"What are you doing?"

I raised my eyes from the wooden table in Tyr's house. Sheets of rain pummeled the roof and windows. Tyr had just come from bed, his short brown hair mussed. Miraculously, though, he wore a light brown shirt, probably because of the draft. "Marking my territory."

He approached to see what I'd done. Too bad about the shirt. His black tattoos looked so good trailing from his neck all the way down to his ankles. Particularly after he'd taken off his pants, revealing the patterns that swirled around his dick, his thighs, his hips, as he drove into me. The corded muscles of his forearms as he held my neck...

The memory of last night made me squeeze my legs together. It was different now, in the not-light of morning and sobriety, but fuck if he hadn't made me come like no one had in decades.

"At least you didn't pee on it," he remarked, frowning.

I smirked, unapologetic.

The comment seemed to remind him. He let out a piercing whistle and opened the door, letting rainwater pour in. The wind fluffed up the braids I'd redone so they sat in place on my head.

"Where did you get the knife?" he asked.

"The kitchen. You really are as dumb as you look."

Now it was his turn to look smug. "You didn't think so yesterday."

"Oh, I did. You can be dumb and good at fucking."

A hurtling mound of fur and teeth barreled into the room, preventing his response. The wolf dripped on everything.

"Fen," Tyr protested, but the creature cut him off with a lick to the face. He pushed it away.

I mimicked Tyr's whistle and stood. "Fen," I called. "You can stay with me."

The huge ears swiveled in my direction and the wolfdog looked at me in surprise. I was struck again by how enormous it was. Half my arm could fit in its jaws, but if Tyr could domesticate it, I didn't need to fear.

It reached me in one bound, shaking the table. I slipped the knife in one of my hiding places, rubbing the wolfdog's head with my other hand. "Fen, is it?" I cast a quick look at Tyr for confirmation. He didn't say anything, but he didn't have to.

I ran my hand through Fen's shaggy, wet fur. It smelled terrible. "How did he get so big?" I could use some of these creatures back home.

Tyr simply gave me one of those cocky looks that didn't need much interpreting.

"Enough," I said. "We're not making everything about last night. Or are you too much of a child to move on?"

Fen's breathing shifted, as though waiting for a command from his master. I readied my gust of air if I needed it.

"He's a Banewolf," Tyr explained casually. "They killed our kind before the earthquake but I wanted to keep this one. Among them, he's small."

"Young?" I guessed.

"Six years."

That wasn't an answer. If Banewolves lived to be fifty, then that was young. If they lived to be ten, then he'd be veering into old age.

Tyr came closer, holding out his palm. "Give me the knife."

"This rickety one that can hardly cut carrots?" I plucked it out of its ill-fitting sheath. "I prefer my own anyway."

"You're not getting those either."

I stood. "Don't attempt to command me. Generations have failed. Armies have broken like water against my will."

Fen's ruff bristled, a subterranean rumble punctuating my words.

"My *gods*, I just meant inside the house. For the next few days." Tyr ran a hand through his short hair. It had a bandage wrapped around three fingers. My doing. The wound, not the bandage. He took his knife back from me. He inspected the tip, which had bent as I whittled my symbol in the wood.

"Then where are we patrolling today? I want to know your... city better."

His eyebrow rose skeptically. "*I* am making my rounds in the god and human sides of town, then *I* am checking the sacred spring before making sure nobody's using this weather to cause chaos on either side of the divide."

In his voice, even that sounded sexy. Or maybe I just liked a bit of chaos.

"You plan to leave me alone?" Even with my war makeup smeared, I knew my feigned look of innocence only managed to look like what it really was—mocking and dangerous.

His broad chest heaved up once in resignation. The movement reminded me of his heavy breathing as he'd dominated me, forcing me to feel every throbbing inch of him. Damn, he was good at that. But, from what I'd seen, he was weak in maintaining order around here.

"You need me," I concluded, heading toward the door. He knew better than to stop me. It had taken him longer than most, but at least he finally understood that no one denied me. In six days, King Hrafnir wouldn't either. I would rule Urd, spending the next month or so getting its citizens in line before...

Here, my mind hitched. *Before going back.* Could I scrape a worthwhile auxiliary force from these bumbling people by then?

This mission had two goals, as far as I was concerned. Neither one was to fulfill my father's godsdamned dream of meaningless conquest. I would offer my people—the people of Eriset, from the humans to the demi-gods—a pause in the eternal fight between the Twin Armies. And then I would use the additional force I found here to destroy my brother until there wasn't a particle left to string together.

The cool mist coming off the streaming rain chilled my bare arms. I cast a glance upward. The sky roiled gray. Where my fortress sat in Eriset, it was arid. We rarely had the gift of water like this. I licked at the heavy droplets before looking back at Tyr. "Coming?"

BELLONA

After picking up one weapon each from the shed outside—the precious ax for him and a dagger for me—we set out into the rain. I didn't point out how easy it would be to recover my belongings and hurt him as he slept. We both knew it. Stowing the weapons was a gesture of peace, and the strongest one I could stomach. My knives were family.

Rain fell steadily, making the turf springy as we walked.

"One of the human settlements first," he said, marching down the ramp to the lower side of the rent. He twisted to look at me. "Don't hurt them."

I raised my eyebrows.

"Please."

I made no promises. As long as these humans behaved, I wouldn't harm them. Did Tyr think I was like Ares, pulling out people's entrails for fun? The insinuation crept under my skin.

It's good if they think you're a maniac. At least for now. Fear made for obedience. Still, I scowled.

We passed a burnt patch of misty trees, and the little path opened up to something more permanent-looking. With the rain, the road was pooled and muddy, but wide enough and packed enough for a cart. The tree decorations here reached up the trunks to human height, as if in apology—ribbons and little hanging bells.

Wooden homes, reinforced with metal, clustered together on the sides of the road. Humans bustled between buildings, checking on firewood sheds, setting out buckets. There were inns and stables. And, gods love me, a wall. About damn time. It wasn't a great wall—just pointed strips of tree trunks bound together with metal ties—but it encircled an inner portion of the human settlement. Runes had been written vertically on the slats. Asking for protection, probably. But there were no guards outside the doors. Protection wasn't passive. It required blood and sweat.

Tyr approached the little portal, small enough that only Fen could enter standing fully upright, and unlocked it with a key taken from a pouch at his side.

The lack of guards prepared me to scorn whatever and whoever I saw for their incompetence. I wasn't prepared for this area to be... nice. Was that the word people used?

Lights burned in glass bulbs strung together between high tree branches overhead. The buildings were small but neat. Cozy, almost. Smoke rose from chimneys, carrying the smell of food. I saw Fen raise his snout to investigate. Through an open window, a woman sold steaming hand pies and baked potatoes stuffed with toppings, the bottom wrapped in paper.

The space inside the wall only encompassed a few streets, but the humans had made the most of them. The hissing mist rising from the rain made everything hazy. Some dream that wasn't a nightmare.

The humans visibly stiffened as we walked by. Some whispered to themselves and bowed to the muddy ground after seeing me. Tyr ignored them. Instead, he paced through the streets, his intense gaze lingering on certain windows and certain people. We passed a shop with a gaping hole in the roof. Water streamed in from above. Even with those signs of destruction, this place didn't seem as backward as I'd first thought. Urd had some potential.

A small head appeared in a doorway, watching us pass, before disappearing. A young woman. I glanced at Tyr. No surprise there.

Tyr talked to a couple humans, asked questions. Nothing, apparently, was unusual. Besides me being there. The trembling humans could hardly speak, their eyes darting between Tyr and me.

Once we finished what Tyr considered a round, we left the way we'd entered. He locked the gate behind him.

"So your house isn't at the bustling center of town after all," I said.

"It's at the center," he murmured, almost distracted.

I rolled my eyes.

The rain thickened as we made our way through the Godlands next. This would surely be better than the little human village. But then, Tyr practically lived in a shack, so my hopes died. The god settlement had no wall and didn't seem half as cohesive. Population-wise, gods seemed to take up maybe ten percent of the total, if I had to guess. Strangely (or maybe not) the style of house was the same as I'd seen on the human side. The dwellings were bigger, but that was just because gods were bigger. Either these new gods didn't know what to do with themselves or didn't have time to create something better amid all the fighting.

Because there had been fighting. The scores and burnt areas didn't end on the human side. Gods had them too.

Compared to Eriset, this was only a taste of chaos. A taste I could manage. Impatience sang through my blood as Tyr repeated his slow look around.

By the time we trekked toward the sacred spring, the downpour was so loud that we didn't speak. Sacred springs were incredibly rare, but it made sense that they had one. How else could they have become gods? The divine concentrated around springs. But that wasn't the only necessary element for deification. The stars had to be in the correct positions. And there had to be a bloody sacrifice. Usually a bull—a human would do, but that practice had rightly faded into dim history. Death didn't only mean cutting an animal's throat, though. Some opted for the little death: public, simultaneous orgasm. The entire ritual was kept tightly secret. We couldn't have humans finding ways to rise to deities.

Nowhere else that I'd ever heard of had created so many unintentional gods at once. It was no wonder they had no idea how to handle themselves. The amount of blood that earthquake must have caused here...

The earth grew mucky beneath our feet. I took out my knife to feel steadier, but I had a feeling this patrol would be a boring one. No other people had appeared during our entire walk. Only the two of us and Fen, slogging between trees through the mud. Life was like that sometimes. Complaining about it was worthless. Action wasn't.

"Tyr!"

He turned, water gushing down his annoyed face.

"Why are we walking the whole way?"

"Horses will just get—"

"Can you not walk through the air? Travel?" I asked, incredulous.

He looked at me, uncomprehending.

I fought not to roll my eyes. I stepped through the air until I stood practically against his chest.

A small intake of breath was his only sign of surprise. Fen coughed an angry bark beside him.

The smell of wet dog and caramelly pine and sharp rain *almost* buried the musky scent of Tyr's body. "Travel," I repeated. This was like talking to a child. How long had he been one of the deathless?

"No, I can't do that," he said, pushing past me up the hill.

No wonder the pace of life moved so slowly here. I strode beside him, water roaring in my ears. "Really?"

"Why would I lie?" he cried, but he showed no interest in knowing more.

"I could think of a couple reasons."

Even demi-gods could travel through the air. If he couldn't do that simple thing, then he definitely couldn't shift. Maybe he could even die. Lucky.

I briefly considered shifting, just to give him a shock, but that was far more taxing than travel. The gods' consensus was not to shift without good reason. That hadn't stopped my father from shifting into gods knew what just to get close to some naked young human. I spit on the ground.

It was pathetic that the gods here didn't know how to step through the air. Maybe I'd show Tyr, since I would be stuck here awhile. For now, that skill gave me another tactical advantage over the deities here, if he was telling the truth.

We reached the spring without incident. It looked like a large, rustic well of dark stone. Unremarkable. But then, most sacred springs were, to look at. Their power lay within. A rumbling in my core responded to the concentration of divine energy. I'd never been particularly pious, like most of the humans and some of the gods were, but I respected power.

Tyr marched in a slow circle around the well, peering out into the empty forest. When he reached me again, he said, almost too low to be heard over the rain, "Fucking guard didn't show."

And here I'd thought they were simply incompetent.

A corner of Tyr's lips curled and he met my eyes. "He'll be surprised to see you pop in this morning to remind him."

I smiled back. Finally, something interesting.

The moment I appeared inside the missing guard's house, my senses went on alert.

The tang of blood.

The back-of-the-throat scent of charcoal.

The furtive sounds of dying movement.

Silence.

I squeezed the knife in my fist and spread my feet, aware of every corner. This house was smaller and cleaner than Tyr's, but items had been knocked across the wooden floor. Tyr hadn't told me the name of the guard who missed his shift at the sacred spring, so I couldn't call for him.

My skin bristled. If a fight came, I'd be ready.

The gods in Urd were new, but that didn't make them harmless. I'd underestimated enemies before and lost soldiers because of it more than once. It was a bad habit.

As I entered a short hall like the one to Tyr's bedroom, my eyes locked on words smudged broadly across the wall in what looked like ashes.

God scum.

Human attackers, then, most likely. That meant this would be easier. Humans were smaller, weaker, and they could die. I sniffed the air. Assuming there had been humans here, they weren't here now.

The burnt smell of charcoal persisted, but we hadn't sensed a housefire in the Godlands. If something had burned, it was small.

I rounded the corner into the first room on the right, knife first. On the ground beside a bed, which he'd evidently fallen out of, lay a half-dressed man—or god, by the look of it— struggling in his own blood. Many wounds. That meant many attackers if my first guess at humans was correct. Though some cuts were already closing, it was obvious that the main weapon used had been knives. The guard was tall and well built with sharp eyes I immediately distrusted. They met my own and rounded.

"I'm not here to finish you," I said calmly, putting my own knife away. I'd seen similar sights a hundred times. "Who did this?"

"You're—"

"Bellona. Goddess of war. I'm sure you heard I was here. Answer my question."

He choked for a few seconds, pale from blood loss, but he'd recover. Gods always did.

"Humans?" I prompted. My pulse surged hot in my veins. If a gang of humans thought they could harm a god in his sleep... If *anyone* attacked a defenseless victim like this, they deserved swift retribution.

And I could walk through air to give it to them.

The guard on the ground coughed hard, blood spurting from his mouth. The whole room stank with it. "Yes," he confirmed.

"Who?"

"There were these two—" At the croaky mention of them, his hand formed a fist against the floor.

"Names."

"I don't know."

This was going nowhere. This guard needed a moment to gather himself. If he didn't know names, then he could give descriptions. Tyr knew a few of the humans. Maybe he could provide an identity after knowing what they looked like.

"Sit up," I said, and went to find a cup. It wasn't difficult, even with the house in disarray. Opening the front door to let rainwater fall into the cup, I spotted Tyr and Fen. I whistled loudly. "Come here!"

I didn't wait for them, instead backtracking to the room where the guard had pushed himself to sit with his back against the bed. Blood smeared the blankets. This time, I saw that a portion of the bed itself looked burnt, but because of the dampness of the day or something else, the fire had never spread.

Tyr entered behind me. He must have left Fen outside.

"Shit," he breathed, hurtling forward to kneel beside the guard. "Vali! What happened?"

"Those two..."

Tyr's jaw sharpened in recognition and rage.

I handed the guard, Vali, the cup of water, curious to watch Tyr react to this situation. I straightened and crossed my arms.

"The two from before?" Tyr demanded, his voice low and

dangerous. A thrill ran through me at the sound. "Where'd they go?"

"Spring."

Tyr was on his feet. "I'll send help for you," he said, casting a reluctant look down at his friend.

"He'll live," I said.

"That doesn't mean he doesn't need help. Look at him!" He turned flashing eyes on me. Rarely did I meet such fearless defiance. I'd let it pass. This time.

"I'm going to the spring to catch these pricks," I announced and left. Even as I said it, I doubted we would find them there. I hoped we wouldn't find the carcass of an animal given in a futile attempt to rise to the status of a deathless one.

"Wait." It was Tyr, who ran to meet me outside the door, where a sheet of leftover rain fell, coating my head. Why had I walked at all? I could have traveled directly to the spring and arrived immediately.

"What?" I snapped.

"Let me," he said earnestly. "I promised that I would end these people if they came back. I want to stick to my word." His green eyes blazed, but I sensed that he didn't relish the idea. Duty, not excitement, lit his face.

"And not let me do it?" I asked. "Fine. They hurt your friend. I understand that."

"Friend." He repeated the word, squinting in confusion.

Fen ambled up from out of the woods. How many beings found him terrifying without his owner to control him?

"Vali's an idiot," Tyr said.

A laugh burst out of me.

"And an unreliable guard," he went on. "But you saw him in

there." He shook his head as we strode quickly through the dripping trees back to the spring. Hints of blue started to suggest themselves between the white-gray clouds. "Terrible."

"You could have fooled me."

He pinned me with a look I felt I was supposed to understand, but didn't. That was unnerving. Normally, I could read people better than this.

"I'm going to send him some help. I'll meet you there." As he sprinted off with Fen at his heels, he added, "If you find them, wait for me!"

Alone, I took the opportunity to step through the slit of air and emerge next to the sacred spring again. Nothing. But at least now it had a proper guard.

17

TYR

After sending a doctor to help Vali, I didn't go back to the sacred spring. Bellona and I had searched there already and found no one. Though she'd done that trick of disappearing in one place and appearing somewhere else, I'd walked the entire distance to Vali's house and passed nobody. The humans who had slashed that maddening, useless guard weren't at the spring anymore, if they ever had been.

Beside me, Fen growled, tense. I was serious when I told Bellona to wait for me to finish off the criminals myself. With her bloodthirsty streak, it was unlikely she would listen.

Why did that couple have to return? I didn't like Vali, but I hated even more seeing him in pain.

The doctor will help. Just keep going.

My rage grew as I approached the border into the human lands. No wonder Bellona had laughed. She had castles and fortresses. In other moments, I might have defended the human population—at least the ones who didn't cause me trouble. I used to be one of them, with the same habits and ceremonies.

Now I felt like one of a kind, not in a good way.

The leader of the human side, a man called Njord, sat at his desk in the public center where I expected to find him. He was a small man with thin blond hair, old enough to remember the earthquake and all it entailed, but only just. I disliked him intensely, but he'd helped me track down members of the Human's Liberation before—after I asked him very pointed questions.

I did the same now. Bending over his desk, I snarled, "I'm looking for two people."

"Lord Tyr." The name came out business-like, although he must have guessed the purpose of my visit.

I described the two of them as well as I could remember from our brief encounter. "They attacked a god."

"Bad, was it?" The same business-like tone. He condoned the couple's actions. It was written on his face.

I ground my teeth, fantasizing about bashing in his head.

Apparently, I didn't need to answer.

"You're sure it was them? Nice couple."

"They bathed in the sacred spring." I knew I was leaning too far forward, blocking out the light of both lanterns by the door. My huge shadow dwarfed him. Part of me enjoyed the flash of fear that crossed his face. "You know the law. I spared them once, a great mercy. Now," I said, my intonation slow and deep, "they attacked a god. Give them to me."

His adam's apple bobbed as he swallowed and made inane movements to straighten parchments on his desk. "Very well.

Germund and Odine Torgrim." The names slurred a little in his mouth. I read that as reluctance, but now it didn't matter.

"Where?"

"East of the fields, by the Brightwater."

I stormed out, stroking my thumb down Peacekeeper's blade.

I RETURNED, BLOODSOAKED AND GRIM, TO THE SACRED spring a few hours later. Hopefully Bellona hadn't taken over all of Urd in my absence.

More than just the Torgrim couple had ganged up on Vali. I never thought I'd have to kill on *his* behalf, of all people. But the message had to be clear. No unprovoked attacks on gods. No unprovoked attacks on humans.

In all, there had been four. I knew this mix of emotions too well. Something like elation at completing a just punishment against the offender, followed by disgust, both at them and at myself for enjoying any part of it. But I had promised the couple I'd kill them if they returned, and I didn't break a promise.

Bellona glared furiously at me when I trudged up the hill to meet her. She stood as straight and imperious as a tree. Even after living so long among gods, she seemed to be made of a different mold—something stronger and more ancient. A power like hers could crumble the world again.

She took in my appearance, the streaks of red on my hands

and clothes, on Fen's mouth. "So it's done?" Her fury softened into something like curious understanding. One soldier to another.

I fell through that look to the one she'd given me last night when she laid down all her weapons. When she'd dared me to take her. That felt like a dream now, one I didn't deserve. But fuck if the memory didn't make me stiff anyway.

"Yes," I said, standing beside her.

"No activity here," she reported. Scanning me with another lingering gaze, she added, "More than two?"

"More than two."

She only nodded. "And I thought you didn't have the balls."

I shot her a sharp look.

She shrugged. "Magnus."

"Death doesn't turn me on," I guessed, angry that she would bring that up. She knew nothing about it. I still thought that drunken fool didn't deserve to die.

"Inflicting pain does." Her eyes turned liquid and knowing.

I flushed.

Something warm touched my neck and I realized Fen was licking the blood off me. I felt a wave of nausea. There were still more rounds to make in my patrol but my limbs dragged with exhaustion.

After a few minutes, Bellona said, "I went back to Vali's house."

"You what?"

"He's doing much better. Very dramatic, your friend."

"He was *stabbed*—"

"And I took a few pieces of parchment." She pressed them into my chest, not avoiding the gore splattered there. I peeled them off and saw she'd written in a large bold script, "Anyone, god or human, who breaks the law or antagonizes others between now and sunrise will be visited by the goddess Bellona."

Visited. But we all knew what that meant. The blood now staining the words *antagonizes* and *goddess* made it terrifyingly clear. I couldn't help but be grateful, despite the huge overstep. In her twisted, violent way, she was offering me rest.

"There are four copies," she explained. "Where shall we hang them?"

Tomorrow I'd check on Vali and see to the other sites I typically patrolled.

Tomorrow I'd worry that Bellona was doing too much of my job.

Tomorrow I'd remind myself that I needed to get her out of Urd.

But not today.

18

BELLONA

While Tyr sponged himself off behind the house, I sat in the front room, idling running my hand against Fen's shoulder. Definitely not picturing Tyr's sculpted, tattooed form, naked and covered in blood and water outside.

In the Eight Realms, humans never attacked gods. It was suicide. Maybe an occasional zealot, but even my memory could only dredge up a handful of incidents in the past thousand years. Never anything on Eriset. But that made sense. The gods were too busy attacking themselves.

I set my jaw, mind wandering to the black makeup I'd surrendered with the weapons. I'd used that little mirror on the pot of greasepaint to disorient many generals. Such a simple thing with such deadly consequences. Now, I wanted it back. My face had to be nearly bare, with faint streaks of darkness around my eyes. I felt fully armored when I had that bar of black over my eyes, like the queen of bloodshed when I painted that stripe down the center of my lips and chin.

Why hadn't Vali fought back? Was he so weak that a handful of humans could leave him choking on his own blood?

Evidently so. I'd felt relieved when Tyr called him a fool. But he'd also helped him. I knew the feeling well. My hand wandered to a couple of coins in my pocket. Hades would be glad to have fewer corpses from Eriset sent across to the Far Realm. It already crawled with human dead experiencing their second life.

Two ideas struck me. A trade. I'd offer—

But my thoughts tumbled momentarily out of order when Tyr reemerged into the house wearing only a small towel, knotted in the front, barely large enough to cover his ass. His short brown hair looked rain slicked and clean. As he crossed the threshold of the front door, he drew a hand absently through it, showing off the thick muscles in his arms. His skin gleamed, the tattooed designs tantalizing, curling around his neck, his pectoral muscles, his thighs, like a living piece of ferocious art. I wanted to scratch and see if they came off.

He heaved a sigh. "There's a bucket out back if you need it too."

It took me a second to understand. "Not now." I almost said something about having servants and several private washrooms at home. The comment would have sounded spoiled, and I was anything but. Half the time, I couldn't retreat to my main fortress at all, but spent my time fighting or strategizing in the field. There were times I would have been grateful for a bucket of water and a sponge.

Fen knocked the side of the armchair with his whip-strong tail as he rose to greet Tyr, who offered him a brief scratch and a tired smile on his way to his bedroom.

I only realized after he'd passed that I hadn't felt annoyed about the casual way he treated me.

I'd been thinking of something...

Yes.

"Tyr!" I called.

In seconds he looked out from the hall, tugging up his pants. Without the belt—it had been silly to give that up—they hung dangerously low. I licked my lips.

"Does Urd have archives of their military history?" *Do you even have military history?*

"Like a library?"

That wasn't exactly what I meant, but if that was all they had... "Okay," I said.

"We have one."

"With military records?"

"Probably. Why?"

And Tyr was the law around here. I didn't bother to hide my disdain for his ignorance. "I want to see it."

His eyes narrowed. "That's not very subtle, Bellona."

I quirked a brow.

"You've made your request already," he continued. "In a few days we'll meet and review it. You don't need to anticipate our movements."

"Oh." I burst into a dry laugh. "I'm not afraid of commandeering your little country. I gave you a week to accept, not decline. To show I'm..." I searched for the word. *Diplomatic* went too far. "Merciful," I said at last.

Tyr's expression declared that he didn't fully believe me. In his place, I wouldn't have either. At least that was one grain of good sense.

"It's a... fascination of mine, different fighting styles." *And I'll use any information or strategy to finally grind my brother to powder.* My gaze dropped to the flame symbol I'd carved into the table in front of me. The sun was setting, sending harsh rays beaming through clouds as though they were making up for being smothered by the rain. One line slashed from the arm of my chair to Tyr's feet.

"What I can't understand," I continued, "is how you've existed so long here when you act like little more than humans." I gave his measly house a pointed look.

Tyr's brow furrowed. "We can't all live in castles. And we *were* humans before. Just because they have no power doesn't mean they're worthless." His tone grew combative, as though he'd had this argument many times.

I enjoyed this side of him—the side that dared to stand up to me. He had no idea how dangerous that was, how many had lost body parts for similar outbursts. I let the moment stew a little longer before responding.

"Humans are what they are," I said dismissively. "But gods should be able to do more. Instead you tromp around, using only your size to your advantage." My eyes dipped to the V below his navel.

For the second time that day, his face reddened.

"I can teach you to travel like the deathless—for gods' sake, even demi-gods don't have to walk everywhere!—if you take me to the library and show me the best materials on your battle tactics." I locked my gaze on his. I hadn't needed to offer anything in trade. But it was too pathetic to see how inept these gods were. Thenios, for all his lecherous idiocy, had been right. Urd was backward.

To my surprise, a bitter smile curved Tyr's lips. "*Now* you're helping us?" His combative attitude had only gained strength.

I stood and met him eye to eye.

"We sent emissaries to the Eight Realms after the earthquake and were sent back with nothing," he growled. "Our differences meant bloodshed across our whole land, thousands of humans killed while we wrestled with what it meant to be something *other*. No one offered to show us what it meant to be gods. We were bigger, stronger. We had stories about different abilities. We knew we couldn't die. But our powers just made everyone else resentful and made the chosen act like they had fucking earned the right to lord over everybody else. The old gods didn't even help. I wanted peace, but both sides were angry and afraid, and it's all I can manage to stop both sides from pulling each other's heads off!" Furious exhaustion crossed his features.

I'd known nothing about those emissaries, and I doubted I would have cared with so many other lives depending on me. Thenios definitely wouldn't have, and they probably only appealed to the High King.

My gut twisted, but I wasn't sure why. It wasn't guilt. It felt like desire, recognition. Someone else was fighting an endless battle on behalf of his people.

I opened my mouth to tell him that it had only just begun, but strangely, I didn't have the heart. He'd discover the truth for himself eventually.

A knock sounded at the door, followed by a voice, small but sharp. "Tyr!"

Tyr broke off his glare with a "oh shit, I forgot!" Fen lumbered toward the voice, no threat in his movements, although some of the hair around his mouth was still dyed red.

Tyr opened the door to reveal a tiny old woman standing very close to the threshold so wetness from the roof didn't drip on her. He and Fen looked huge by comparison—warriors compared to a child.

The woman looked even smaller when her attention shifted from Tyr to me. She fell on her face in reverent terror. "Your Majesty." Her words muffled against the ground.

Tyr turned to look at me, an accusatory warning in his eyes. I gazed levelly back. I had no intention of harming this woman. If I did, she'd already be dead.

Her bones seemed brittle to be pressed into the dirt like that. "Rise," I said. What was she doing here? I had little cause in my normal life to meet an old human. Most in Eriset didn't live so long, and the deathless didn't age. This woman's lined skin and pinched eyes elicited a morbid curiosity.

"Come in," Tyr murmured. "I'm sorry I forgot our tea."

Tea?

He drew his big arm around the woman's shoulders and ushered her inside.

"I apologize for the interruption, Your Majesty," she said to me.

"When have you ever apologized?" Tyr replied, amusement softening his features and tone now. Turning his attention back to me, he said, "This is Hild." He inhaled as though to say more, to explain who she was to him, but he only closed his mouth.

"You know who I am. Your mother?" I guessed.

Their faces both fell a fraction. "A friend," Tyr said.

"Best friend." I liked the glint in the woman's eyes now that she realized I wasn't an immediate threat to her.

I looked up and down from Hild to Tyr and allowed myself a tiny smile. Best friends? I'd never seen an unlikelier pair. One was a tower of tattooed muscle and the other was a frail old lady who barely rose to his middle. Fen was taller than she was.

"She can stay for tea now, right?" Tyr's question was for me.

I left him in suspense for a few moments before relenting. I wanted to know more about this woman. "Make it for us."

Hild grinned, nervous excitement radiating off her as I indicated for her to sit in the filthy armchair. "Thank you, Your Majesty."

I cast Tyr a smug look as he disappeared to fetch us tea.

"I didn't know you'd be here," she said, her veined fingers clutching the armrest as she lowered herself down. Fen nudged the side of her head and she harumphed, suddenly grumpy as she pushed him away. She didn't appear to be afraid of the beast. Registering something slimy on her fingers, she looked to see bloody saliva. With a swallow, she merely wiped her hand on off on the skirt of her gray dress.

"How do you know Tyr?" I asked, stepping away so I didn't loom over her so forcefully. Behind me, fire started crackling in a little stove.

"We patrolled together, before... everything happened." Her eyes rose to the patch on the wall, the one with a crossed ax and branch. A relic of his past, then.

"But you didn't ascend."

She gave me a wry look. Some of the iron I'd witnessed in Tyr reflected in her gaze as well.

"I thought gods and humans didn't fraternize here," I commented.

Her face flashed angry, though not at me. "Tyr and I do. He's a good one."

Good. What did that even mean in a situation as convoluted as this one? Most humans wouldn't consider what he'd done today *good*. But I, and apparently this odd little woman, understood it.

"I..." The woman licked her dry lips, searching for the words. Or maybe searching for a way to make the wrong words sound less offensive. "I'm very surprised to find you here, Your Majesty."

"I'm staying for the next few days until I can assume a greater residence."

"Tyr invited you?" Hild eyed me skeptically.

"The king suggested it."

At that, she blew a breath out her nose. Fen took the sound as an invitation to lick the side of her head. "Get off! Tyr, he really is too big!"

No sound replied from the kitchen, but it wasn't difficult to imagine his smirk.

"A guest like you..." Hild resumed. "Of your stature." As she spoke, the truth seemed to crystalize in her shrewd gaze. She knew why I was here. Or part of it, at least. "I'm glad they allowed him the honor of hosting someone as great as you."

I swallowed my own smirk at that. Tyr had fought the command, but we'd both made the most of it.

So my first impression had been correct. Although Tyr worked for peace, he was granted small recognition for his efforts, even disciplined for appearing to choose sides. His outburst a moment ago made more sense.

Hild couldn't hide a grimace as she took in the small, tattered space, obviously not improved or thoroughly cleaned in years. "Forgive him," she finally said. "This place is a pigsty."

I chuckled. "We should tell him."

By the time Tyr returned with a pot of hot tea, I decided I liked Hild, and I liked Tyr more for liking her too.

❦ *19* ❦

TYR

I set down the teapot and pulled a couple more chairs against the thick table, urging Hild to take the tallest one. She said she preferred the armchair.

Her immediate prostration in front of Bellona had reminded me of the terrifying deity she was. Something had jolted painfully in my chest.

Was I not taking Bellona seriously enough? Would she ever consider hurting Hild, a weak human who couldn't defend herself anymore?

In my brief absence to fetch the tea, as Bellona demanded, Hild had become remarkably calmer. In fact, they spoke warmly, if Bellona could be said to speak warmly to anyone. Her sentences weren't all commands. The flinty aura of threat she always wore had dissipated like the rain.

Bellona and I sank into seats beside each other, Hild small as a troll in front of us, yet I had the odd feeling that she had gathered us, the two gods, to take us to task. The situation and the earlier kills left me almost lightheaded. I poured myself tea and gulped down a scalding mouthful. I looked down to see the others staring at me.

"Tea," Bellona said, gesturing to places in front of her and Hild.

I poured it, handed it out. These commands were a delicate balance. I didn't want to upset our equilibrium, but I also wasn't used to taking orders.

"And half dressed," muttered Hild into her cup, her gaze both chastising and amused.

I frowned. This was how I usually looked. I wasn't going to change everything about myself to appease Bellona.

When my mouth fell open to protest, she shrugged. "It was cold today. I thought you'd have more decency."

These women had too much in common. As I scowled and reached for more tea, I wished—almost as much as I wished not to be conquered by the Eight Realms, a fear I stuffed too deep to feel—that Hild had become deathless too.

After a while, even with Bellona there, our tea wasn't too different from the way it usually went. The goddess was quieter than usual, listening. What she was listening for, I didn't know. Once I ignored that unnerving presence, however, Hild and I fell back into our old rhythms. I made a second pot, and it was full dark by the time Bellona and I walked her home.

Nighttime in Urd was a hushed blackness when only trees spoke. We didn't erect lantern stands anywhere but at the main port and in front of the meeting house and spring. I wanted more, but getting them was a task always left for tomorrow.

So, I was left in blind darkness with the queen of war. Her

footsteps, despite her height and thick muscle, were all but silent when she wanted them to be. The short candle in my hand did little more than provide a vague frame of reference for the next step. I knew the way like I knew my own body, and even Bellona seemed to understand the layout of major areas already.

"Stop," she said.

My ears perked, on alert. I saw nothing. No glint of eyes in the darkness, no rustle out of place.

"You're going to travel."

I exhaled. "Like you did. Disappearing?" The idea sounded ludicrous, and I was tired.

"You're a god." Candlelight underlit her face, making her a fearsome apparition. "Act like it."

"I don't—"

"Do you want to be able to protect Hild? Vali?"

My silence turned stony.

"Give me that." She gestured for the candle. I handed it over. "Picture the inside of your little house. Hild and I agree it's like a sty."

"My gods..."

"Picture pulling the space in between toward yourself until it folds flat against itself."

"Do I close my eyes, or...?" I had to admit that the possibility of doing this excited me, but the pressure from having such a teacher made me wary. What if I couldn't do it, and she considered me as weak as the king did, an unfit ally?

"If you need to." Only the slightest tinge of mockery laced the words.

After fixing her with a pointed look, I closed my eyes,

doing as she instructed. My front room appeared before me and I imagined dragging it toward me.

"Mm hm," she said, the sound low and approving in her throat.

The noise threw off my concentration for a moment as I recalled other sounds she'd made in her throat as I'd possessed her on that bed.

With effort, I focused again. "Pull the space toward you," I repeated, mainly to stop my thoughts from careening to last night again.

"There's a tightly packed space now between you and the destination. Step into it quickly, with resolve."

I paced forward a step. Something wavered in the air, pressing in around me for a moment before bursting like a pocket of mist. I opened my eyes, turned, and faced Bellona again. Still in the forest.

She materialized in front of me, still holding the candle, which had whiffed out during the jump through space. A faint curl of ghostly smoke rose from it. The darkness, complete but for the light of the moon and stars, didn't bother her at all. "Try again."

It was the kindest response a warrior like her could have given to my failure. I repeated the steps. This time, the squeezing sensation grew until I could hardly breathe. With a gasp and a few rapid blinks, I realized I still hadn't moved.

"Did you feel anything that time?" Bellona asked.

"Yes," I said. "I couldn't breathe. What is this supposed to feel like?"

"Like that," she replied lightly. "But it doesn't last long. You're only going to your little cabin."

Clamping my jaws shut to prevent a retort, I straightened.

Front room.

Pull the space toward myself.

Step through with intention.

I held my breath this time. Hopefully, that would preempt the horrible drowning sensation I'd begun to experience last time. The world pinched around me and I was insubstantial, lost in a crack of space too small to bear. Panicky now, I leaned forward, toward my vision of the room.

My shoulder hit hardwood as my lungs filled with air. I gulped it gratefully.

My house. I was back in my house. I'd done it. Elation replaced the panic and I stood. Bellona, silent as a shadow, stood there too. She set down the cold candle near her symbol on the table.

"A lot of drama for one small jump," she commented, but I saw the smile threatening to curl her lips.

Questions gushed out of me. "How far does this work? Can you do it as many times as you want? Do you have the know the place you want to go?"

"In time," she said. Now there was no mistaking the gleam of pride in her dark eye.

I'd put that there. The goddess of conquest approved of several things I'd done today.

Somehow, though, my favorite moment had been watching the banter between her and my oldest friend. Bellona didn't despise or dismiss Hild because she was human. They acted almost like friends.

The goddess was undeniably formidable in her primal

ferocity, but there was another side too. I was growing to enjoy both the terror and the competence.

When our eyes met again, warmth sizzled between us. My gaze dropped to her full mouth. Could I make her scream again, surrender to me?

She placed a palm flat against my chest. Her calloused fingers felt chilly from the night air. Gooseflesh rose around her touch.

"Get some sleep," she said. "We go to the library in the morning."

A dismissal. My blood cooled. What had I thought—that I'd have her every night? The very idea sounded hopelessly naïve. I wasn't used to feeling young, but this goddess had been tempered by centuries. To her, I couldn't be more than a momentary distraction or an obstacle to be converted to an ally.

"Good night then," I said.

Her hand dragged down my skin to rest at her side.

I turned toward my bedroom alone.

20

BELLONA

I spent all morning pouring over books and parchments in the small library of Urd. It had none of the grandeur of the Archives nor the vast options of Scira's famous collection, but it had something new. I hadn't read anything truly new in a long time, and I soaked it up like a dying plant soaks up rain.

Urd's historical volumes mixed legend with fact, poetry with figures, but even that unnecessary complexity whetted my appetite to discover the truth and, along with it, hopefully something I could use against Ares when I returned. My brother was violence and force, not finesse. He didn't study battles like I did. These meager, crumbling papers in this dank stone chamber fed me. Their ink became warpaint on my fingers.

This was why I was here. It wasn't to strike up a fling with a minor god who might cloud my judgment.

I had recognized the look in Tyr's eyes last night. Admiration and desire. But he had a job to do and so did I. We both needed to be sharp.

I'd once gone ten years without a fuck so I could channel every ounce of energy on ripping my brother's claws off Eriset's second most important city. Once I did it, the next month was a haze of sex and blood and drink—all the things I'd denied myself to achieve that victory.

My situation now wasn't as desperate, but I saw an opening to gain more ground, so I would take it.

The library, once I avoided the epic poems and love stories, held mostly old records of human conflicts, not deathless ones. Still, no advantage was too small. Axes and arrows were their preferred weapons. Soldiers also wore swords, but since those were common across nations, I paid less attention to their ideas about that.

Battle fury was a common phrase. The will to win. It was that, more often than expertise with weapons, that won them battles against their northern neighbors. Coupled with their knowledge of the woods, which made for ideal surprise attacks, battle fury won the day.

The candle had burned down to the stand by the time I rose, stiff from craning down to read. These stories provided more than strategy. They were a window into the society that had created them, one that prided itself on its own wildness, revered the forests, and held itself to a strict, though somewhat foreign, sense of right and wrong. It was a brutal culture, distinctly aware of death—in that way, not unlike my own.

Right now, I wasn't sure if any of this would be useful to me, but I tucked facts away like weapons for retrieval.

Something tapped behind me. I spun toward the sound. When I saw it was King Hrafnir, his good eye dull in the dimness, I raised an eyebrow. "Coming in for research?" I asked dryly.

I'd only slipped one of my many knives into its sheath before I left Tyr's. Stupid.

"You could say that." He indicated the pile of paper I still held in my hand. "You too, I see. Did you learn something?"

This felt like a trap. "There's limited knowledge to find."

He still hadn't moved from the doorway. His lips pressed in acknowledgment. "You may take a few, if you like. When you go back to Eriset."

Ah. I had no intention to tell them I meant to go back at all, not before I ruled this place. "I'll take them anyway, gracious king," I ground out, tucking the sheaf of papers under my arm. I'd been about to set them down when Hrafnir entered, but I'd take them with me now.

His eye narrowed. "Very well. Lord Tyr, he's treating you well?"

Why all this inane small talk? "It's adequate. Enjoy your reading." I plowed forward, forcing the king to move out of my way.

"Queen Bellona," he said as I passed. "We both know Urd is not worth your attention. Your own country—"

I whirled on him. "Don't speak to me about my own country!"

"And don't presume to know mine."

I clawed my hands before remembering that I didn't have my godsdamned gauntlet on today. I missed those deadly fingertips. His brazen response left me flushed and murderous. But I couldn't murder him.

Not yet, anyway.

He had five days left to decide whether or not to obey me, and every day he stalled meant another day of quiet for my people.

If he refused, *then* I'd have to kill him.

"*Your* country? You belong up north, don't you?" I goaded. Tyr's story about how Hrafnir, for all his experience, didn't help the new gods boiled my blood.

"I belong wherever I am, Queen Bellona."

A raven swooped over our shoulders and settled on a forked candlestick amid the books. It looked at me with piercing intelligence.

"Funny," I said. "I've always thought gods ought to earn their place."

"There's truth in that too." Hrafnir shook out his sleeves a little. I was getting sick of his coded, sage-like talk.

Without another word, I stalked out of the building and back toward Tyr's house. Everything in me screamed to retaliate. It was as natural as breathing, but now I had to hold my breath. I should have said something more, but anything that passed my lips would have come out as a curse or a threat.

My vision had blackened with rage by the time I reached the shed in the back of Tyr's house and yanked my gauntlet back on. All my other weapons slipped dangerously into place. Warpaint streaked across my face again and I breathed, drawing a thick line down my chin.

My identity was growing hazy here. Even a trip taken in relative peace had its dangers. I would never be safe. I would never be free from struggle. Sometimes the fantasy of a restful day made me angry at night. I didn't want a restful life, but a few hours? Hell, yes.

I marched inside, dumped the papers on the table, and shredded a new gash in the armchair before flinging myself down. I wanted to hurt something.

That was where Tyr found me after it had grown too dark outside to see.

He stumbled out of nothingness, a second of panic replaced with triumph. At the sight of me, fully armed and glaring, knees spread wide, nails scraping up the fabric of the armrests in rhythmic strokes, his eyes rounded. He spread his feet as though a fight would be even.

I sighed, gesturing for him to stand down.

His muscles relaxed, the tattooed ridges not quite as defined. "Tough day," he guessed, his tone careful.

I blinked slowly in response. The king's coyness had been nothing at all. So why was I still angry? I rubbed the aching spot in my chest.

"I got you something on the way home."

I frowned, sitting up. "What?"

From his pocket he drew a small round pot with a fitted lid. Its design reminded me of Tyr's tattoos and of the traditional Urd symbols I'd seen at the Great Hall.

"And here I thought you were happy to see me," I murmured halfheartedly, rising to get a closer look. Was it a trick? Why would he buy me this?

When I didn't touch it, he took off the lid. Shiny black paint, fragrant and waxy, filled the container.

"What is it?"

He gestured pointedly to my face. "I thought you'd run out."

After the rain yesterday. Most of the warpaint had rinsed

down my cheeks, leaving dark splotches around my eyes and streaks of gray along my neck.

I puzzled over the gift. It didn't fit into my world. If this had been an offering from a fearful worshipper, I would have understood. But a gift? Not demanded?

I took the pot of paint and replaced the lid, my previous anger hollowing out into something that ached differently than the pain in my chest. I couldn't name the feeling. Grief came close, but wasn't right. I wasn't grieving. All the same, a small lump formed in my throat. I swallowed but it lodged stubbornly in the center.

"I didn't run out," I said, closing my metal fingers around the little jar as I held it against my stomach.

"Okay. I was on my way and I just thought... but that's fine." He raked his fingers through his hair—gods, I liked when he did that—and moved past me toward the little kitchen. "I'm starving," he announced. "I think it's a night for meat."

"Rare," I specified.

When he was out of sight, I gazed down at the gift in my hand. It wouldn't go into the shed when I finally found sleep. It stayed with me.

❧ 21 ❧

BELLONA

When I woke, I was angry. That wasn't uncommon, but I couldn't remember the reason this time. Was it Hrafnir's dismissal of me in the library? Their scanty information on battle tactics, now strewn over the thick wooden table in Tyr's front room? The attack on Vali, the spring guard, two days ago?

The wrath against my brother was a constant. No, at this moment, something else burned in that sore spot behind my collarbone. This wound felt fresh as an arrow puncture. Only when I saw Tyr emerge, sleepy, from his bedroom did I understand.

I followed him into the kitchen.

He eyed me warily. "What's wrong?" he asked, giving me his full attention. Wise.

I thrust the little jar of black paint against his bare chest. The feel of the gift under my palm sent a new wave of anger through me. It hurt.

"I don't accept bribes," I said clearly. "And this was a poor one." I hated that he'd managed to thaw the thick layer of ice surrounding me last night. I'd been weak, and I was never weak.

When he didn't grab it, I let it fall to the ground. Unfortunately, it didn't shatter.

His brows tilted downward. "Bribe?" His voice still sounded thick and gravelly with sleep. I could feel how warm he was compared to the cool air even from here.

"Letting me stay here, playing tea party with your friend, and now this? I don't change my mind once it's chosen a course. I will have your little community, and I hope your king isn't fool enough to oppose me when his time's up."

Now annoyance flashed in Tyr's eyes too. "What are you talking about?" He glanced at the pot of warpaint rolling along the floor. "I got that as a thank you for showing me that traveling thing. And I thought you might be out. I'm not committing a crime by being decent. Is it that rare that anyone is kind to you?"

I snarled. "Don't play the saint. I know you don't want me to succeed here."

He pursed his mouth in a line, eyes darting over my face as if debating something. "Of course I don't want you to conquer my city, but I understand it might be inevitable because you're Bellona, the fucking goddess of war. I want to know what kind of society will be left, and I hope"—he fixed me with a stare—"you'll find room for gods and humans. That you'll truly help us. I don't like bribes either, especially when they're promises no one intends to keep."

We glared at each other, breathing hard. He smelled musky

from bed, and primal urges reared up again. I had nothing left but primal urges, apparently.

"It was a fucking gift, Bellona," Tyr finally said. "That's it." He bent down to pick it up and slammed it onto the counter.

Warpaint. Something that didn't soften my edges or mold me into something other than what I was.

I was hasty, angry, because the truth was too complicated. Pain made sense. Rage made sense. I wanted to hate him for how he made me feel—whatever this roiling mass of emotion was.

"Did you feel sorry for me?" I asked, riling up my own anger again.

"Sorry for you?" he snapped. "That's the—"

"She has no makeup." My voice grew taunting.

"My gods, Bellona!" I could tell he wanted to push me, hold his hand over my mouth. Something. "Can you not—"

I released a puff of air that sent him stumbling backward.

"What the fuck?" he roared, advancing.

Yes, come closer. "Don't want a bit of fun?"

"This is fun?" He was livid. His face had flushed all the way down past his collarbone, highlighting the black designs on his neck. I wanted to bite into them. At his sides, his hands formed fists. Those beautiful muscles tightened, ready for a fight.

I wouldn't give him one. I might not want to care about him, but I cared enough not to obliterate him.

"Not yet," I said, a mix of challenge and seduction. "You want to show me how wrong I've been, how angry I make you?"

His gaze went dark with lust as he understood. "Yes." His voice was a midnight whisper that sent chills up my back. After a few heavy breaths, he said, "Turn around and put your hands on the counter."

I obeyed.

His next exhale came heavier. Maybe he hadn't expected me to do it. For this to be just another way to torture him.

"Lean forward." This was a god used to speaking in commands. I liked it. "Face down." All my skin responded in waves of tingling. I pressed my forehead into the countertop between my hands.

I felt him position himself behind me. Desperate fingers found my waistband. Pulled. My knife belt was in the shed so there was no resistance as he stripped the pants down my legs.

"Spread wider."

With the leather around my knees, I couldn't move much. He smacked my ass, hard. I bit back a cry of pleasure and tried again.

I hardly had time to hear the rustle of fabric before he plunged inside me, deep and punishing. He was already rock hard. He thrust so wildly it was as though he was trying to slap me with his body, not just possess me with his cock.

I leaned over further, pressing back into him, relishing the sting where we connected, daring him to do more. I'd had so many years of violence, so many years of sex. *Make me feel something.* My mind flitted to the little jar. *Just not that.*

Slowly, he bent over me, our bodies melding together as though he would whisper a threat in my ear. Instead, he ordered, "Look right."

I turned my head. He forced three fingers into my mouth. With his body pressing down above me and inside me now in two places, dark pleasure bunched in my core, spreading outward. I savored it and I savored him. He tasted like dirt and salt and blood. I sucked his calloused fingers hard, pulsing my tongue around them. I met his eye as he watched, his jaw going almost slack enough to open. The dark green of his irises had gone nearly black.

Bold of him to assume I wouldn't bite him.

Unless he wanted me to.

His other hand found my hip. He gripped hard and used it to jam himself more fully into me, grinding against my ass and releasing a grunt of effort as he let go.

I sucked his fingers as he pulled them from my mouth.

"Fuck you," he muttered, but a slight smile shone in his eyes.

"I hope so."

He straightened and renewed his furious pace. One big hand descended on the back of my neck. He knew the pressure points, even at a new angle. Where the blood and air flowed through. He cut them off. My center grew wetter, more sensitive to every movement inside me. That subterranean scream I needed filled more of my body. Pieces of it escaped my lips, hoarse around his harsh grip.

He watched me greedily. "Yes," he murmured, half frenzied. He gave a particularly violent thrust. "That's... it. Scream."

I let the scream take me, clenching and shuddering as it escaped. His fingers relaxed, holding my neck loosely for the sound to find purchase on the air. My noises came out both high-pitched and guttural, ragged. When I came to, he was finishing, pulsing heat into me with uneven, eager shoves. His groan could have made angels turn sinful.

My body sagged as the high from my orgasm faded. He slid out of me and I straightened.

Before I could drag my pants up, he caught my chin in strong fingers and turned me to face him. His earlier fury had faded into tired, pleasurable irritation. For a moment he didn't say anything, and I let him hold me there, facing him. I was a little surprised he wanted to say anything. I let him have his way with me. Most would have chugged a cup of water and gone out to work.

"What the fuck is wrong with you?"

Morning light painted his cheekbones and strong jaw red. It was an honest question, not the kind of bullshit comment hurled by an aggressor. I almost twisted away, but in the wake of what we'd just done, I didn't want to give him the satisfaction.

Sometimes, this backwoods god of battle almost made me care. Caring led to pain and distraction. I couldn't afford either when I had only a few days left here to secure additional troops for defeating Ares.

"I prefer your body to your pity," I replied.

His top lip lifted in a silent snarl as he let go. A twinge of regret surged behind my belly button. He felt dirty, I was sure of it, and not in that enjoyable, feral way.

I swallowed and hauled up my leather pants. Tyr glanced around the little kitchen distractedly as though searching for food before shaking his head, slamming a palm on the counter, and leaving.

The pot of war paint tipped over from the force.

That had been a nice, quick fuck—nothing earth-shattering, but good nonetheless—so why did I feel like shit?

22

TYR

I couldn't stay with Bellona anymore. I'd lose my mind. That fucking goddess was in my head. One minute, I thought we were allies and the next, I wanted to kill her. Or she wanted to kill me. And then the ferocious way I'd taken her this morning... I couldn't think straight, kept imagining places and ways I could command her, bring her to the brink of falling apart. The wet heat of her sex, the way she wanted me to dominate her in those moments, the power I felt when I did...

But that control was an illusion. Bellona held all the power, not only over me but all of Urd. If the king thought he had a decision to make, he was kidding himself. The goddess was as unpredictable and indomitable as the ocean. Our connection, if I could even use the word, was like the beautiful, terrifying surges before a storm—hypnotizing, but ultimately deadly. Bellona wasn't a friend. She was barely even a lover. She was a conqueror, and I happened to stand in her way.

Hopefully, I wouldn't encounter any troublemakers today. I was in no mood to show mercy.

Nothing at the sacred spring. Vali had already mostly recovered from his attack, but a different guard watched the landmark now.

Nothing by the coast, where some of the poorest human settlements were.

Nothing near Hrafnir's house since Magnus had broken in.

Nothing, nothing, nothing. A boring day, but in my world as peacekeeper, that was a good thing.

Fen kept me company, but even he was on edge. I had to keep an eye on him around the humans so he didn't spring forward and attack any of them. He obeyed me, but my own mind was so murderous that he could easily mistake my seething brain as permission to do violence. Keeping him in check gave me something to focus on.

The only new development I sensed was the way some looked at me. Stares of fear and accusation followed me on a normal day, but today there was a shift. I knew without asking that word had gotten out about Bellona's threat to conquer us, and that she was staying with me.

I was a traitor, those looks said, siding with a foreign conqueror, the queen of bloodshed.

I met each one of their glares, one hand lightly on Fen's back, the other on Peacekeeper's haft.

That afternoon, I finally returned to the Great Hall when I knew King Hrafnir would be sitting in audience. He didn't look surprised to see me, even with Fen still at my side. Normally, the Banewolf knew to wait for me by the door, but today he followed me in like the embodiment of my anger.

"Lord Tyr," the king began from his throne.

Before he got out another word, I cut him off. "Queen Bellona has to stay somewhere else."

"Excuse me?"

"I don't care where. She can bed down in the forest for all I care, but she has to leave."

"There are still four days before our meeting," he replied, as though that settled it.

"I know, but making her stay with me has painted me out as a traitor to our nation. She's volatile. I won't have her in my house." My face heated with rage.

"You are no traitor, Tyr," the king soothed. "I commanded it."

"Yes, but—"

"It is because she's volatile that I chose you."

And because you wanted to punish me for being too soft on the humans...

"She hasn't caused any destruction since she's been here," he continued. "I commend you."

I scoffed. If she hadn't destroyed anything, that was the result of her choice alone. I had nothing to do with it.

Hrafnir's voice lowered a fraction. "You can help her see that we do not need her here. She seems to think we require her supervision. You can prove otherwise."

I swept my arm in a broad gesture. "I can't convince her of that. She's conquered dozens of cities in her time. My word won't change her mind, I swear to you."

"I will not have her causing havoc elsewhere. She certainly can't stay here."

Hrafnir's home was one of the only ones big enough to

house more than the inhabitants that lived there. A stab of shame pricked me at that thought. We were poor. We were barely keeping our feet here.

But I couldn't suggest she stay with the king. As often as we disagreed, I wouldn't throw him into the direct path of Bellona's violent unpredictability. My job was peacekeeper. Deadly certainty settled over me that I couldn't kick her out of my home. Not until this was all over.

Better me than anyone else. I'd just have to do my best.

No more gifts, even perfectly innocent ones.

"There is no change in my command," Hrafnir concluded.

I inclined my head, though inside I was roaring. A growl rumbled up from Fen. I spread my fingers to calm him.

Through gritted teeth, I answered, "As you wish."

Four more days. Just four more days. If I kept my distance, maybe I'd keep my sanity too. In the meantime, I'd do my job and pray that Bellona would rule justly when she inevitably took over the nation that was my home.

FOR TONIGHT, I WOULDN'T BOTHER GOING HOME. HRAFNIR was wrong. Nothing I did or said kept Bellona in check. Hopefully, she wouldn't burn the place to the ground when she realized I wasn't coming back. At this point, I barely fucking cared.

After I was dismissed, I charged through the forest, using my newfound ability to jump to the edge of what I could see ahead of me. Jump, jump, jump—Fen struggled to keep up with my speed. I stumbled less often now. The speed was dizzying, freeing, gave me back a little bit of the control I tried so desperately to maintain.

Bellona had stripped that from me from the moment she arrived on our shores. My credibility in front of the king, the threatening persona I needed to cultivate for gods and humans to take me seriously, and my nation. She'd taken all of it. Any semblance of control was hers. It didn't matter that our sex suggested the opposite. That was just another way she controlled me—my thoughts, my body. Shit, even the memory of driving into her made me half-hard again. I ran faster. Maybe I could outrun the chaos that swept all the order I'd painstakingly created into a mangled pile of char.

The only good thing to happen today was that traveling wasn't difficult for me anymore, not over short distances anyway. I held my breath and stepped through. Easy as that. None of that panic and stumbling remained from the first time. But my limbs had grown tired from exertion by the time the sky began to darken. Had I eaten today?

I shoved away the memory of the kitchen with a growl and observed my surroundings. My thoughts screamed so much louder than the forest that I hadn't observed as closely as usual. Beside me, Fen panted heavily. He was tired too. Absently, I rubbed his head, looking for a place to stay. I'd slept in the woods plenty of times, during the war especially, but my stomach begged for a hot meal.

Hild's house wasn't far. I headed in that direction, walking this time so Fen didn't need to sprint to keep up. A tug of guilt snagged my brain. I'd forgotten our weekly tea and now I was about to ask her a significant favor. At least this was Hild and no one else. She'd say something snarky and set about making food for Fen and me. I'd failed in front of her more times than I could count. Although our differences only grew more pronounced, she understood me in a way no one else did. She understood if I needed to take violent action and she understood when I chose to show mercy instead. Even the gods didn't grasp my job as fully.

The patch on my wall reminded me that someone believed in my mission to keep peace between the aggressive factions here. Someone cared.

My anger gave way to hunger and eagerness to spend time with someone who wasn't me. In front of Hild's little house, half-sunken into the ground, I knocked.

No answer.

I waited the space of five breaths and knocked again, harder. Fen sat obediently beside me. He looked eager too, even though the dusk made it more difficult to distinguish details. His eyes looked black as a raven's.

Finally, the clatter of a lock.

"Who...?" Hild appeared through the sliver of doorway, eyeing me like some witch in a story. When she saw who it was, she widened the door to let me stoop and enter. "Tyr! I was just about to sit down to soup and read some naughty stories. What are you doing here?"

I felt my face relax. "Do you have anything hardier than soup?"

She scowled at me. "Would you like me to provide a menu?"

"If you have one."

She cocked her jaw and waved her hand at me as she turned to go deeper into the house, as though I were a pesky fly. "Leave him outside."

It could have been my imagination, but Fen looked abashed. I pointed and gave a sharp whistle. Fen reluctantly backtracked out the door. I closed it behind him.

"Thank you, Hild!" I called. She was no longer in sight. "I'm sorry to drop by with no warning."

Her small form reappeared around a corner. "You know it's no trouble. Well," she revised, scrunching her forehead and looking at the ceiling, "you're always trouble, Tyr, but you're family. You're always welcome."

I cleared my throat.

A thought seemed to occur to her. She stiffened, looking around, taking stock of what she had. "Is the goddess joining us?"

"No," I said firmly.

"Thank the gods!" she said, visibly relaxing. "*Your mother*. Please!"

I followed her into the kitchen. Hers was even smaller than mine. Until Bellona, I hadn't realized how almost everything in Urd was still human-sized, as if we gods hadn't accepted who we were, hadn't grown into ourselves yet.

She caught my eye, unhooking a ladle and stirring the pot of soup she'd evidently been in the middle of preparing. At a glance, there wouldn't be enough for both of us.

"Problems between you two?" she asked.

"Besides her declaration that she's the new queen of Urd?" When Hild didn't release me from the death grip of her stare, I sighed. "If I'm trouble, she's..." But I couldn't think of the word. I didn't want to say war. Yes, that was her specialty, but I hated the thought of that for my nation. Not again.

Hild turned back to the stove. "Do you know what her plans are?" This time, her question came out a little quavery, like an old woman's.

She is an old woman. I didn't know why it struck me as improbable every time I saw her.

"Let me do that." I moved into her space and she had no option but to step aside. I commandeered the ladle and stirred, on the lookout for something else to fill my growling stomach. I'd pay her back when I could.

"I'm not incompetent, you know!" She placed tiny fists on tiny hips.

I ignored her and gave the soup a sniff. Potato. Everything went with potato. I just had to find...

"I thought you were getting along, all things considered," Hild resumed.

"Me and Bellona?" I frowned. "I thought the same of you. But you do have some similar qualities."

She smacked my arm. "I hope you mean her attitude that refuses to take shit from anyone."

I nodded. "I didn't mean her height."

Another smack. "And you didn't answer my question. What is she going to do? You've spent more time with her than anyone here, it seems. You have to have some idea."

Her real question rooted itself in real fear. A fear I had too. *Will she destroy the humans?* Her reputation declared how blood-thirsty and ruthless she was in battle. It wasn't difficult to picture her eating the heart out of enemy chests. Maybe she bathed in blood at home to renew her perfect skin. Hild's question was a good one—I just didn't have any answers. The goddess wasn't exactly forthcoming. Or kind. Or reasonable.

Heat flushed my cheeks as I flashed back to the night before. For the briefest moment, as I gave her the black face paint, Bellona had looked vulnerable, unsure. Her composure snapped back so thoroughly that I wasn't sure I'd seen it at all.

Now that I stood here with Hild, unclenching the fist that had held my anger at Bellona's chaotic, irrational outburst this morning, I knew for certain what I'd seen. A goddess with no friends in an endless war. Maybe my simple gift that hadn't been intended to bribe or woo was the first like it in years.

That didn't excuse her belligerence this morning, but a part of me liked this theory. It fit the otherwise insane pieces. I'd seen enough people act violently out of habit, old grudges that no longer made sense. Vulnerable people, like the human population or gods who felt they'd been insulted, were often the most dangerous.

Maybe if I could simply comfort—

I laughed through my nose before the thought finished. Bellona didn't want or need comfort, and even if she did, it certainly wouldn't be from me, the conquered. Even in bed, she wanted war.

"What?" Hild asked. I had almost forgotten she was standing there. "Is she going to make our lives a party, then?" There was an edge to her tone now.

"No," I said, sobering. "I don't know what she plans to do, but... I don't think she'll harm the humans." How could I be so certain she would keep her promises? Somehow, though, I felt she was telling the truth.

Hild took a breath and scanned the room, obviously

looking for something. I followed her eyeline to a string of onions. "I think I have some—"

A loud snarl and piercing whine cut through the air, slicing away her words.

Fen.

I bolted to the front door. As I approached, many voices spoke chaotic directions to each other outside. How had I not heard? I flung the door open, heart hammering.

A crowd gathered around the door. The closer people backed up when I burst out. They were all armed, wild-eyed. But all I could see in the torchlight was Fen with two thick arrows in his side.

23

BELLONA

I sat in the tatty armchair, legs wide apart, leafing through the reams of parchment I'd taken from the library. So much of it was drivel. At the time, I hadn't looked to see what I'd taken. Half of it was poetry with barely discernable themes of conquest and dying well.

The second wasn't a luxury I could ever have.

I was down to the last couple pages. None of this could help me lay permanent claim to Eriset. Twirling a knife between my fingers, I heaved a frustrated breath.

After Tyr left this morning, I focused some of my remaining emotion by shaving the sides of my head. They'd gotten fuzzy in the last two weeks. The scrape of the blade against my skull calmed me. I'd done this hundreds of times. The action kept me sharp and my profile recognizable. Even from a great distance, no one doubted who I was. The piled braids, the black bar across my eyes, the leather bristling with knives...

A line on the page caught my attention.

Urd is a warrior society, but the civil war caused such devastating loss among humans that it no longer keeps a standing army.

I stared at the page. No standing army? This fucking society had no standing army at all? How did I not know this? Their small number of pitiful gods—I thought of Vali—wouldn't be enough to turn the tide against my brother.

I roared and upended the table. Seriously? I'd come all this way, too far to even travel between realms without a ship to take me part of the distance, and they couldn't help me defeat Ares?

Why hadn't Tyr said anything? The logical thought bled through like a miniscule light in a raging storm of darkness: *You never told him your plan.* I cursed myself and then him.

I'd been blind. At some point in the past few days, I would have seen evidence of an army, but instead all I saw was a disorganized pack of lawless individuals. No wonder Tyr felt the entire burden of keeping order. No wonder he was crumbling around the edges. Neither the gods nor the humans had a military.

I ground my teeth. What was the point of coming here at all?

The truce. That was it. Just a break in the fighting that would erupt again as soon as I headed back home. Our eternal fight would continue as it always had. The Twin Armies clashing in a spray of blood. Innocents caught in the crossfire or targeted by my depraved brother.

Heat filled my cheeks as I tried to calm down, but my body was shaking.

No standing army.

The document was recent enough to have referenced the

war between gods and humans, but was that still true? I thread of hope—no, not hope, desperation—tied me to the idea of checking with Tyr. Maybe in the past couple years, some group in Urd had realized the stupidity of having no organized defense force and reestablished the army.

I took measured breaths. Leaving the table on its side, I stalked outside to get a sense of the time. Research consumed me in a way that devoured time as well.

Dark. Tyr should be back, or at least on his way, but I didn't hear footsteps.

He had been angry when he left. I didn't dwell on the thought. Anger was nothing new to me, but in its wake I felt as though I deserved it. That sensation was much rarer.

Was he not returning tonight? I saw nothing as I peered into the darkness.

My eyes couldn't adjust properly to the blackness, so I'd shift into something that could see better. I'd find him and get the information I needed.

I didn't often have an excuse to shift. An unspoken rule among gods was not to shift without good reason. I'd never been good with rules, but that one was ground into my blood. I simply didn't think of shifting most of the time because others didn't. Now, though, I had a choice.

Tyr could be anywhere. There were many places to search and I wanted to find him quickly. The solution arrived, bright and obvious.

With an inhaled breath, I looked up and spread my arms, feathers blossoming along their length. I contracted into something smaller, more compact but still deadly. My feet grew talons, and I tucked my legs under me as I darted into the air.

A falcon.

Now the shapes of living things became clear, even through the dark trees. I soared on silent wings high enough to scan whole areas at once. Humans and a few gods milled about their various business or pleasure, holding lights, but no Tyr.

A commotion reached my heightened senses. That was a good place to look. I veered right and found a large group gathered around a little house.

I knew that house. Tyr and I had walked to it after having tea with Hild.

I swooped lower. The mob outside Hild's house was jostling, fighting, brandishing weapons. There were maybe fifty of them, mostly human. Two stood above the rest, though. Gods. Interesting.

Facing them was the enormous figure of Fen. Even from here, I could see his teeth bared, his fur bristling. Were they trying to kill the wolfdog? My heart beat faster. I alighted on the top of the house. If they touched him...

Fen snatched the nearest human by the arm, pulling him irresistibly closer like a shark with its prey. Bones cracked as he finished him. A grisly way to die.

Arrows flew, thunked into flesh. Fen released a sharp whine and slumped to his side. Air caught in my throat. Where was Tyr?

Before I could shift back to mow down these insurgents, he erupted from inside the house, ax drawn. His eyes lighted first on the injured Fen. With feral rage, he hurled himself against the group of attackers, but they seemed to have been waiting for just this moment. Their yells grew louder, more personal, more obscene. They wanted Tyr, not Fen.

I took a few self-indulgent seconds to watch. When Tyr had killed those humans, I hadn't seen him do it. His fighting skill was all talk until this moment. Now, I could see what he was capable of.

He killed the first two humans in a stroke, their bellies sliced open. He parried an attack from the side and managed to fell another man.

"Get back!" he roared, planting himself above one of the corpses. "Get back!"

Most didn't get back. A couple even ran to finish Fen off.

Hell no.

With a screech, I darted from the roof. Talons pierced and scratched the men's faces. Their screams confirmed I'd hit the mark. Warm blood spurted against my feathered breast.

With another inhaled breath that felt like a deep stretch, I took my own form again beside the fallen body of the wolf.

For a moment I did nothing, just let dread coat the assembled mob when they saw who it was. Bellona, goddess of war, queen of bloodshed.

I couldn't tell if it was relief or terror or anger in Tyr's expression when he looked at me. All I knew was that the look was bright, intense.

Those closest to him were the first to move, lashing out as if they knew they didn't have much time to accomplish what they'd come here to do. They were right. They didn't.

Tyr shouted in pain as someone hacked at the hand holding the ax. It dropped. The mob's movements became a frenzy, a storm with Tyr at the center.

I traveled close enough to touch Tyr and stepped back through the air to Hild's front door where I'd stood a moment before. Two attackers clung to him. I slashed at the first, cutting his throat. The other ran. With a burst of wind, I sent the entire group tumbling backward end over end, tangling, yelling. The torches flickered wildly. One flung backward and the flame caught on the trunk of a tree.

"Don't," said a voice, but the bloodlust was on me.

I marched forward with long strides toward the nearest enemy, unsheathing a second weapon. I laid the point against his chest, watching his eyes widen in terror before plunging it in. I didn't let him suffer. The second thrust was to his neck.

"Don't!" the voice cried again. "Stop, Bellona!"

The men were scrambling to their feet now. Some bolted through the trees. I stepped through the air to appear in front of one of the cowards. He screamed as I gutted him.

"Bellona!"

Finally, I listened. It was Tyr. I stalked back slowly, aggressors scattering in my wake. The fire licked higher up the tree now.

"No one tells me when to stop!" I bellowed, then gestured to the fleeing enemies and mangled bodies. "Are these friends of yours?"

He sneered, bloody chest heaving. "They don't all need to die." His voice was quieter, but no less commanding. His brow was low, eyes flashing. Blood streamed down his right hand. From the compulsive tremors of his throat and the lines around his mouth, I could tell the wound hurt.

We both turned to Fen at the same time. His paws and ears made little movements. After shooting a glare at Tyr, I went to the Banewolf's side. The crushed body of the man he'd killed lay beside him. I knelt and placed one hand on Fen's shoulder. He bucked at the touch, snarling and writhing.

Tyr knelt beside me, speaking soothing words. Fen stilled, though his breathing was still jagged. From his side protruded two thick arrows. I met Tyr's gaze. Fen might not make it.

I felt along Fen's furry ribs toward the wound to determine if the weapons had pierced anything vital. Medicine wasn't my specialty, but anatomy did fall under my purview. He flinched as I got closer to the arrow.

"Shhhh," Tyr soothed, petting Fen's flank. Whatever he was doing did seem to calm him.

One arrow embedded itself in the meat of his shoulder—nothing deadly there except the possibility of infection—and the other seemed to have missed the heart and lungs. No guarantees, but I could probably save him.

I wiped my gory knife off on Fen's fur and looked at Tyr. "Get meat or something he can eat," I ordered.

He eyed the knife warily without moving.

"Now!"

"Hurt him and I'll see to it you never rule again."

As though he could make good on that threat. I jutted my chin toward the door.

A small spike of gratitude tore through me as I remembered whose house this was. At least Hild hadn't been harmed in the fighting. She'd been wise—shrewd little thing—and stayed indoors.

Tyr sprinted in and out within seconds, Hild trailing cautiously behind. Her eyes blazed at the sight in front of her.

"They were after me," Tyr explained to her in a rush as he returned to my side. In his hand was a small loaf of bread.

"I said meat."

He matched my glare. "She doesn't have any."

I closed my mouth. Tyr seemed to understand what I was doing because he positioned himself at Fen's huge head while I stayed by the arrows. The wolf's head stretched with interest as he sniffed the loaf.

"Give him a little," I muttered, poising the knife next to one arrow shaft.

The small distraction didn't stop him from howling in pain as I sliced into his shoulder to dig out the arrowhead. I pried it out, gory and dripping, and cast it aside before placing my hand over the bleeding wound. The arrow had missed major arteries, so I felt safe moving onto the second.

Fen whined through his nose. I hated the sound, but it wasn't as if I'd never heard it before. Setting my teeth, I repeated the action with the second arrow, managing to wrench it out too.

"This is why we needed meat," I said over Fen's sharp cries.

Tyr's throat bobbed. He didn't even look at me, his shining eyes locked on Fen's terrified face.

I turned to Hild, who'd silently watched the whole thing. "Something to wrap the wound," I ordered.

With a final grimace, she returned to the house to obey.

When I looked back at Tyr, something twisted in my chest. "I'll help your wound too."

He raised his brutally sliced hand as though he'd forgotten all about his own injury. After a moment, he lowered his brooding eyes, and grunted a quick "thank you." He looked exhausted, devastated. This attack had been personal, even after all he'd done for them. A fresh wave of fury washed over me. Maybe I should have killed more of them. I would have, if Tyr, the one they targeted, hadn't wanted me to stop. How could he still harbor any compassion for these people? They'd attacked him.

And I had a strong feeling it was because of me.

24

TYR

We dropped off Hild at the house of a cousin of her late wife. That crowd outside her home looked ready to set it ablaze and I didn't want any of the survivors to return and take vengeance on her for being my friend.

After Bellona bound the wounds, Fen was able to limp along beside us. We walked, slow and tortuous, back to my house. I had little to say to her. I hadn't asked that she run in and save me. Hadn't asked her to kill those men. But when she materialized out of nothing, terrifying and deadly, I had to admit I was grateful. Especially when she helped with Fen.

None of that changed the fact that the mob probably wouldn't have formed in the first place if the citizens of Urd didn't perceive me as Bellona's ally. We weren't allies, but our display tonight would solidify that perception in people's minds.

I chewed my lip, my sliced hand throbbing. It was useless

to point out that my own home might be a pile of ashes by now. Bellona showed no fear or hesitation. Darkness, blood... those were her territory. Before her arrival, I would have said they were mine as well, but her level of violence exceeded mine.

She held aloft the candle that Hild let us borrow. It flickered against the newly shaved sides of her head.

When we finally reached my house, I wanted to fall into bed and sleep for days, drown out the confusion and exhaustion, but Bellona ordered me into the armchair. Her metal fingernails had scraped new lines along the top of the armrests. My table lay on its side. I couldn't muster enough feeling to be surprised.

Bellona went outside and carried in the bucket of water I kept out back. Thunking it at my feet, she crouched and took my wrist in practiced hands. "It's already closing up," she announced.

I nodded. I'd been stabbed before and worked through it like a passing disease, highly uncomfortable but never deadly.

She picked up the rag draped across the edge of the bucket and dipped it in the water. With a squeeze, she wrung it out and methodically wiped off my hand still dripping blood. The blade had bitten deep into the flesh just below the wrist. She acted with all the tenderness of a doctor used to seeing much worse injuries. Still, another pang of gratefulness threatened to bubble up inside me.

I wasn't grateful to her. I couldn't stand her. She was actively tearing down everything I'd fought to gain, everything I'd built around myself to give my new immortal life meaning.

"I thought you hated me." My first words surprised me.

Her eyes snapped to mine. "I don't hate Fen."

I tipped my mouth. I liked that about her, damn it. Only Hild and now Bellona accepted my Banewolf as something lovable. In an odd way, that gave me hope.

She positioned my elbow on the armrest so the injured hand rose above my heart. Rising to her feet, she said, "Do you have a standing army?"

I glowered at this change of subject. "No."

"Shit," she breathed.

"What? Did you want to kill them all too?"

"I thought they could be helpful in taking down my gods-forsaken brother," she bit out, staring at me in challenge.

"Ares?"

She blinked with the exact effect as if she'd rolled her eyes. "Obviously. Did you think I meant Lox?"

Pieces clicked into place. I sat up straighter. "Is that why you're here? To get more people to fight for you?"

"It's a good thing you're pretty."

"Enough," I growled, standing to meet her eye. "Enough insults for me and my country and my people. I know you could somehow obliterate me if you wanted to, but I've had enough. Thank you for saving Fen. I'm going to go bind my hand. If you want to inform me of your plans in the morning, just don't wake me. I'll be asleep." I had no strong liquor in the house or else I would have pounded down a few glasses before leaping into bed. Today had been hell.

Bellona regarded me as she would a puzzle. All condescension left her expression. As I turned to leave, her mouth opened.

For some reason, I waited to hear what she would say, but she just stood there. She didn't look like a violent goddess now. She looked... almost human. Not quite vulnerable, but a little unsure.

After a moment, I gave a wry, humorless smile and made again to leave.

"This is the last of it."

"What?" I snapped.

She sniffed and raised her chin, but the gesture didn't portray that stone-hard confidence she usually had. "I ran out of warpaint today." She met my eyes, and I finally understood that she was talking about the streak of black across her face.

I raised both eyebrows laconically. "Okay."

Her eyes glinted with something else, something unsaid, but it didn't reach her lips. Her thick arms flexed uncomfortably.

She wasn't going to say anything. I might want her to apologize, to make beautiful promises about the safety of the land, but she'd never say those words. We were creatures of action. And her actions left me so confused my head spun.

I sighed and trudged heavily the short way to my bedroom.

I CHECKED ON FEN FIRST THING IN THE MORNING. Underneath the wrapping, his wounds still looked fresh, but not infected. Whatever Bellona had done last night worked.

Without telling Hrafnir, I decided to take the day off. I

hadn't done that in... how long? It felt like ages. Probably more than a year. My mind and body reeled, and Fen needed me to keep an eye on him.

We didn't discuss it, but Bellona stayed here too. I wished she'd gone out somewhere—I would be much more comfortable alone—but she acted as if I needed a guardian. I hated to admit it was a welcome change, if only for a few hours. I was always the protector and now she shouldered that role.

The mob might come for me again. Or, they would, if Bellona didn't stay conspicuously in sight of the open door polishing her weapons.

It was a bright, warm day, and I spent the morning righting the house. Not only was furniture upended but the place was filthy. Hild and Bellona hadn't been wrong. My mood became steady as I went through the motions of cleaning and thinking about what had happened the past few days.

Only three more until the king's decision. What would happen if he refused Bellona's demand? I hated to think. I had to talk to him about it and convince him to strike a deal with her, one that meant everyone could still live as they were, one that spared King Hrafnir too. A move like that wouldn't earn me any friends, but it could save lives. That was the point of my job, wasn't it?

In the meantime, I'd sow more of those ideas in Bellona's mind too, so she'd be ready to accept his offer.

Her revelation last night about using us to help win her war came as more of a surprise than it should have. I didn't know how to feel about that, except that the Eight Realms weren't my country, so I had no interest in fighting their battles.

Would our lack of an organized military give her excuse to leave us alone?

That seemed unlikely. She was still here, after all. She could have left while I slept. I'd risen after the sun today, which was out of character.

Besides a few passing comments, we avoided speaking to each other. Whenever I looked her way, though, she was usually watching me. Her presence was as big as Fen's, every move she made the result of a hundred years of practice. The potential in that impressive body kept drawing my eye. It wasn't only the fierce lines I remembered touching, but something more. It was like looking at a great waterfall. I knew getting close could crush me, but awe drew me forward against my will. She was a terror, but she had layers and layers of life I had only begun to understand. One of those layers, though she'd never admit it, was tremendously lonely.

I knew what it was like to fight a losing battle alone. Finding Fen had been a stroke of divine luck.

And it didn't matter that she was lonely. She was also cruel and lashed out at anyone who attempted to care. To be a god was to be lonely.

I knew I should use this opportunity to ask for her clemency on my people, but the right words wouldn't form.

I brought a few cuts of meat and loaves of bread to the house where Hild was staying. I kept the neck and heart to give to Fen when I returned. He looked up gratefully from where he lounged in the midday sun. I scratched his favorite spot behind his ear. He leaned into my hand, which had already healed most of the way, and twitched his paw at the rate of my fingers.

Thank the divine I hadn't lost him. I glanced through the open door. Bellona wasn't sitting in the spot where she'd spent most of the day. Strangely, I wished she were, so I could lock eyes with her fierce ones to thank her for saving my friend.

25

BELLONA

"What are you going to do with the bodies?" I asked, polishing the last knife to a shine and placing it with the others. I'd begun that morning—sharpening weapons calmed me. Now it was early afternoon and we'd worked together in silence for an hour or so.

Tyr hadn't gone out as he usually did. Maybe the encounter rattled him. The mob outside Hild's house was unfortunate, especially for Fen and Hild herself, who would definitely have been killed if we hadn't taken swift action. But the skirmish had been brief and decisive. Nothing to cry over now.

"There are body men," he said across the table from me, oiling his own blades.

I raised a brow for him to go on.

"They take care of the bodies from any conflict—bury them."

"You don't send them to the Far Realm?"

He frowned, looking puzzled. "Far Realm? No. We bury them so the bravest souls can join the divine."

My lips quirked. What a nice, easy notion, made sultry by his deep, accented voice. "What happens to those who aren't brave?"

"What you saw, I guess," he said, cutting his eyes away from me. "Brutal, short lives with nothing after. I try not to think about it."

"When you're mowing them down?"

"Some people deserve it."

I hummed. Experience had shown me that was true. "Did you see the gods in the crowd too?"

His lip curled and breathing deepened in disgust.

"Anti-occupation?" I guessed, lilting my voice.

He set his jaw.

"Not that it matters now anyway." I began tucking the smaller weapons into the folds and sheaths of my clothes. I'd even polished the little poison flask.

Tyr watched me with a trace of hunger. For my prowess, my body, or what I didn't know. Maybe he just wanted me to take my weapons back outside.

"Will you spare the humans?" he asked suddenly.

My brow lowered as I looked down at where he sat. "The ones who attacked you yesterday? Doubtful."

"No, I mean the rest. The humans in general. Some gods think we'd be better off without them, or using them for labor." He looked like he wanted to spit. "They're people too. They deserve a place in this land as much as we do."

I regarded him for a while. He didn't look away. "I'll spare the humans. Most of the humans." I tucked another knife into a pocket on my thigh. "I don't burn cities at random, like the rumors say." I couldn't help but get quieter. I liked those rumors.

"Do you bathe in the blood of your enemies?" An almost teasing note entered his tone.

"Why? Do you want to join me?"

He swallowed, the tattoo at his throat sliding at the movement, and looked down. "I do need to know. If you'll help, like you promised, then I won't oppose your rule. The king hasn't been perfect but he's a being of great wisdom. His focus has just narrowed to one side of the divide. I'm sure he'll bow when it comes time."

Begging for his king's life. I wouldn't have expected him to do that. My observation had shown that Hrafnir and Tyr didn't get along.

"You plead for mercy a lot for a 'god of war.'"

His eyes snapped up to meet mine and he stood. "I don't plead for mercy."

I smiled. "You were. Just now. And last night, when you begged me to stop."

"You've seen me covered in blood more than once and it's been—what?—four days?"

"Who isn't covered in blood now and then? When we bathe, for instance." My eyes trailed down to his strong chest. Picturing him bathing was a treat.

He grew solemn, thoughtful, pinning me with those deep eyes. "We're fighters," he said. "We kill and punish. But what's the point without protecting something? There's no satisfaction in killing without limit. I guess I do show mercy sometimes, to gods and humans." He paused, searching for words.

"I'm trying my fucking hardest to be fair, to stop everyone from hurting each other. I'm exhausted. So, yes. Sometimes I'm wrong when I kill and sometimes I'm wrong when I show mercy, but I'd rather show mercy and be able to fix it later than the other way around."

My experience with the true god of war had taught me something different. Ares showed no mercy. He sought out innocents on purpose.

Tyr wasn't self-obsessed like my brother, reveling in the killing itself. His was a different kind of warfare. His explanation tasted like meat and wine. I liked it, wanted more.

"Maybe you should be called the god of justice, then," I suggested. "Not war."

"Maybe." He moved his broad shoulders as though he were trying on a coat and found he liked it. He checked my face. "Are you mocking me?"

"Amazingly, no."

Tyr wasn't a coward, yet he could pull back when violence called its siren song. He stood up to me—something few beings had done and survived—yet recognized that my overthrowing the nation was as inevitable as sunrise. I wasn't called conqueror of cities for nothing.

I liked him, maybe as a general. He'd be a valuable asset back home. He could make sure I always had a supply of warpaint. And Fen could come too.

"So you won't destroy the king?" he asked.

The warm bubble that had been growing in my chest, a welcome reprieve from the usual pain there, deflated. "I haven't decided."

Tyr and I hadn't really fought, despite our disagreements. I didn't want to have to over this.

"How's Fen?" I asked.

"Better." The word came out tight. He didn't accept my change in topic. "You say you want to help—"

"I like order, so I will help put your backwater kingdom into shape."

Tyr laughed, humorless, as he slung his ax into his belt. "Bullshit. You like disorder so you can eliminate it."

That so perfectly captured the truth that for a moment I stood stunned. How had this young male pegged me so quickly? His intimate knowledge made me defensive. I pushed down the rising instinct to strike. But I used his voice in my mind to do it.

Tyr was in my head. His words, his problems, his ideas, his body. I gravitated toward him as though he were far more important than he was.

Could I get rid of his influence?

Did I want to?

Vulnerability was death. It didn't matter if I secretly liked his stupid gift or felt interested in what he had to say. Or that I wondered what he would do if he knew all of me because I suspected he'd be fascinated. Or that I wanted to know more about him.

Oh shit.

"Fine," I said, pushing past him. My bare arm grazed his side. It felt warm and solid and dangerous.

Shit shit shit.

"Maybe you're right." I didn't look at him as I headed out the door to check on Fen, whose massive head rose to greet me. The wolfdog's tail thumped the ground as I crouched beside him.

I can't enjoy this. To care about anything meant opening myself up to more pain.

But I already knew that if anything happened to Fen or Tyr, I'd go feral. A hole would be ripped in my bloodthirsty heart.

Shit...

I was falling for the god of justice.

TYR

Since Bellona wouldn't promise to spare King Hrafnir a horrible fate, I had less of an idea of what to say to him. Hrafnir, despite his faults, had sacrificed much to lead us (or at least the continent as a whole), and we weren't an easy people to lead.

Gods healed, yes, but there were many legends of gods being endlessly tortured. We could feel just like any human. The idea was unbearable. Personally, I'd much rather die than lie dying but not dying of thirst while birds plucked out my innards.

Bellona had the power to create more order if she wanted to, but the part of her that craved blood, craved chaos... I couldn't trust it.

My plan had been to convince Hrafnir to accept her demands. With time running out, he needed to make a decision in only a couple days. But now I wasn't sure what to do. The mob and then my interaction with Bellona had set me on edge. Maybe they were right. Maybe I was getting too close to her—an invader, an enemy. Fraternizing with her, even at the behest of the king, almost cost Hild her home and her life.

I stopped and looked up. The Great Hall. My feet had taken me here almost despite myself. I had left Fen at home to give him another day to recover from the arrow wounds. At least he could walk today.

With the limited information I had, I still needed to talk to the king. He probably wanted to say something about the demonstration the other night, anyway. I pursed my mouth at the idea. I wasn't in the mood to be criticized by people on both sides of this tug for power.

Steeling myself, I went in.

And my heart stopped.

Splayed on the floor were bloody bodies, so violently mangled it was as if they'd been pulled inside out. Wet blood sheened the floor. Nausea surged in my gut and I almost lost my breakfast. I'd seen vicious attacks before, but nothing like this.

Peacekeeper flew into my hand, but whoever had done this wasn't in the main room. My palm felt clammy.

I didn't recognize anyone.

Wait...

That one had an eyepatch.

Splashing over to him, I knelt. The king, King Hrafnir, lay eviscerated but cruelly still alive. I finally realized the others were gods of the court too. People I'd known my whole life. Who could do this? *Why?*

Being a god wasn't a blessing. It was a curse.

I wasn't a comforter, but I tried to give Hrafnir a heartening look as vengeance screamed to replace the horror inside me. I would find who did this. I would find them and swoop down like the violent god I was. Whatever revenge I was capable of, I'd visit on the dogs who had done this. This evil had to be answered.

Rising, eyes burning, I scanned the ground, searching for prey. These butchers would not escape my wrath and the sooner I could unleash it, the better. Otherwise, I feared I would incinerate.

Bellona should be here. I wouldn't hold her back from the worst punishment she could devise.

A shoeprint in blood led around the corner. My pulse pounded so heavily my chest hurt. I'd felt anger, but never hatred so deep. Picking my way around the scattered bodies— all still alive, all struggling—I stalked toward those shoe prints.

But before I reached the edge of the growing pool of blood, someone rounded the corner toward me.

Someone tall, with bloody shoes and a huge bloody sword. Brown leather crossed over his massive chest. Red paint smeared his brutal face and his shorn head.

Ares.

My blood froze. Ares was the monster of my childhood. His silhouette and wanton violence were even more famous than Bellona's.

Ares had done this? Ares, the Eight Realms' god of war himself?

My mind couldn't wrap around the reality of this. What had Bellona said? She wanted us to help her in the war against Ares. And here he was, bringing the war to us.

I tightened my grip on Peacekeeper, but my fingers felt like wood, my skin and muscle like clothing that could be taken off. If Ares did to me what he'd done to these others, how long would it take to heal? Would Hild survive an occupation like this? No. There was no chance. Not unless I defended her.

Ares gazed at my battle-ready stance and didn't bother to take one himself, though he still brandished the weapon he'd used.

"Missed one," he said, and smiled. His clipped accent, exactly like Bellona's, slithered down my spine. He was glad, *glad,* to have another victim.

Rage filled me like a hurricane until I could barely see. Curses choked me so thoroughly that none came out. I charged.

My attack didn't even seem to concern him. His dismissal only made my attack more furious, more frenzied. I hurled my ax forward, aiming for his meaty sword arm.

A stomach-swooping jerk sent me sliding across the slick floor, weapon flailing. I saw the bare part of his leg just above the knee and struck out as I fell. He stepped back, out of reach. And was my ax... bending?

Before I could jump up, Ares knelt on my chest so hard I felt my ribs creak. I hadn't even seen him move. Gasping, I writhed, but he held my arms down. My arms were thick with muscle but Ares' hands were massive and immovable as stone. I'd never felt something like this. Ever since becoming a god, I was the tallest, the strongest, the biggest. Ares was a level above me and there was little I could do.

I spit in his face.

He licked his lips with a predator's calm. I bared my teeth

in disgust. At my expression, he smiled again, leaning harder. My breathing became little sips—it was all I could manage with his weight on me.

Could I travel away from here, like Bellona had shown me? One attempt told me it wasn't possible. I wasn't upright so I couldn't step through the air, and I needed focus I didn't have.

Peacekeeper lay near me, but the metal blade had warped into a blunt ball.

"I got a little excited when I arrived," he said, his poisonous breath hot on my face, "and I forgot to ask about my sister. You know where she is, don't you?"

"She went back to Eriset." I hated that my voice wasn't stronger, but I couldn't get any air. I tried again. "Where she will destroy you and everything you ever thought to care about."

Hopefully, it was true. I wished I hadn't balked at her idea of having us help her in the war. I'd gladly hurt Ares and his minions in any way she directed. If lying about her location would help her do that, there wasn't even a decision.

Ares breathed a laugh, his eyes going dark and manic. "Centuries of trying haven't gotten her anywhere. She isn't in Eriset. Where is she?"

The implication was clear. Speak or experience unspeakable pain.

I ground my teeth, glaring up at his red-streaked face.

I'll heal. I'll heal. But it was Hild I couldn't get out of my head. An occupation by Ares would leave none alive, and she was already so frail. My resolve wavered.

Bellona was my only hope. She could stop her brother from

destroying Urd completely. I had to believe it. Her ferocity matched his, though his depravity far outstripped hers.

I braced myself for the first blow. But it didn't come.

When I met Ares' eyes again, my bowels turned watery. He wasn't going to simply flay me and leave. Judging from the smile playing on his mouth, he was going to take his time.

BELLONA

A ship. There was a ship in the harbor. And it had red sails with the symbol of a spear.

From my vantage point atop a hill, the red shone clearly through the trees. Nothing else had been that exact color while I'd been here. There was only one explanation— Ares had come to Urd.

A familiar rage filled my veins like fire. Where was he? And how dare he come here? Had he changed his mind about taking it over himself? I shouldn't have been surprised. The truce was only between the Twin Armies in Eriset. Thenios had said nothing about enforcing a truce if we fought over Urd.

Fuck.

The idea set my pulse pounding. Urd was mine. I'd offered to overthrow it to give my subjects a rest, to gather more strength for a victory against my brother. And now here he was.

He would do as I'd done, probably look for the leaders, if

he didn't carve a bloody path of civilians for fun. At the thought of Tyr, whom I hadn't seen for a few hours, my entire body burned.

I was wrath. I was death.

I tore my way through the forest to the meeting place.

I should have known! It was just like my brother to fuck up my plans and show up causing destruction just where I didn't want him. He took joy in it. This scenario was too familiar, but now our war had spread to the Beyond.

No. Not if I can help it!

I didn't encounter anyone on the way there, which was odd. Had everyone hidden in their houses? They'd know who Ares was since many recognized me.

No sign of human causalities. I stepped through the air into the meeting house.

Coppery blood, glistening in the light of the torches, covered everything. There were one, two... eight bodies of suffering gods ripped open in his signature style. I took a slow breath to stop myself from shaking from the force of my anger.

Ares himself knelt in the midst of the carnage, pinning down another victim.

Not just another victim. Tribal tattoos curled around the wrists Ares held down. My throat spasmed.

Tyr.

I flew forward, not thinking, not seeing, just doing. He'd gone too far. I'd send him to Abaddon at last, where the fucking maniac belonged.

Knives gripped in both hands, I collided with Ares a

moment after he noticed me, knocking him off balance. He leapt up, graceful as a panther.

"Ah," he said. "I wondered where you were."

An inarticulate cry ripped from me as I attacked—knives, metal-tipped fingers. I was a creature of power and claws. Sparks flew from our clashing weapons, sizzling in the blood on the ground. Now some of it ran down our bodies. Wounds somewhere. They'd heal. With my adrenaline, I didn't feel them, lashing out at the red marks on his smug face, the arms that had pinned Tyr to the ground.

"Nice to—" Ares grunted as I landed a blow. "Nice to finally play together after so long. You and me."

He enjoyed this, the sport of it. I bared my teeth and whipped out a longer knife. I hated him with more of myself than I thought existed.

Tyr no longer lay in the corner of my vision. I hadn't realized I was watching him until he wasn't there. I jumped forward, stabbing Ares deep in the shoulder and blowing him hard against the wall before leaping back. When I hazarded a turn of my head, Tyr stood beside me, holding a club that had been his ax.

"Out of the way," I snapped.

"No."

There wasn't time to argue. "Then don't miss."

Together, with renewed fury, we attacked. Ares had no army behind him this time. He was one god against two. I could hurt him. We could really hurt him. My desperation transformed into the battle fury all those books talked about—the excitement, the frantic energy. Eager for blood, I struck. *We* struck.

I landed a deep cut to the place where his neck met the shoulder. His expression hardened into hatred. I felt a horrible laugh build inside me. All my training and years of struggle and maybe, finally, here—

Tyr screamed, but by the time I turned back, Ares had disappeared.

I sucked in a breath, looking around.

"Ares!" I shouted, but he didn't reappear. *Coward.* "Fuck!" To Tyr, I asked, "What did he do?"

His grimace revealed his pain. The slice to the hand the other day hadn't hurt him much, so this had to be more serious. He rotated so I could see.

His back and side, red with blood, had been cut open in a long gash. I was used to god-wounds. With binding, this one wouldn't take too long to heal. Not like the rest of them lying like corpses. Their recovery would likely be a year.

But seeing Tyr in pain, even pain that would eventually subside, did something to me. Every sound and smell and touch felt magnified. Even time seemed to bend and stretch, racing then slowing to a crawl.

I gripped his arm and stepped through the air, taking us back to his house. Blood dripped from his wound onto the wooden floors. He didn't have his weapon anymore. Maybe he'd hurled it at Ares and my brother took advantage of his twisted position. I felt like a fool for not knowing exactly what happened. I knew for certain, thought, that Tyr hadn't run. With a cautious bark, Fen trotted up to the closing door.

Tyr and I locked eyes. I knew without him saying a word that he knew what I was doing.

"Stay here," I ordered. He'd know enough to bind his back while I was gone dealing with my traitor brother.

"I can—"

The rest of his protest faded as I traveled away.

I was tempted to go toward Hild first to make sure she was safe, but that would reveal another weakness and I already had too many of those. Where would Ares have gone? He didn't know the area well enough to materialize anywhere strategically unless he'd headed back toward the ocean.

I raced through the path he must have taken to the Great Hall, skipping ahead at a dizzying rate, nearly colliding with trees.

There!

"Ares!"

From just inside the tree line from the beach, he turned to face me. The slice near his neck bled down his front, matching the paint on his skin. None of his arrogant complacency remained. Even that small movement, of turning, spoke of threat as loudly as a coming tidal wave might. His eyes flashed with the hatred I felt.

A few small human figures darted away in my periphery. No bowing this time. Good. It was time to run.

"Crawling back home?" I sneered.

"Fucking in the mud where you belong?"

Air felt sharp in my lungs, but he'd said worse things to me, so I forced myself to calm down enough to think clearly. "You were a fool not to bring your army."

He prowled closer. "Even if you'd cut off my arm, I wouldn't be worried about beating you."

I stood my ground. I lowered my voice to a sinister

murmur. "Then why haven't you when you've had hundreds and hundreds of years to do it?"

The rage in his expression gladdened me. Here was my enemy, the only one I sometimes feared, although I'd never tell a soul, and I'd hurt him. I'd angered him. Without his armies, he was just another opponent. Sure, years had thickened his muscles and war had taught him how to fight, but that was true of me too.

"I'd rather see you suffer," he whispered. In the past century, I'd seen this level of honesty from him maybe one other time. We encountered each other at a key border city after a particularly ruthless day of fighting and even he had been too worn out to put on his smug, urbane exterior. This was the truth beneath.

"I know," I said, lip curling. *Come closer*. "Why bother with these new gods when you can have me?"

He took another step. A dreamy sheen passed his dark eyes, overshadowing the hate he felt for me. "So many gods at once, and their screams tasted so good." His fingers flexed on the sticky sword hilt.

My insides writhed. "You're a sick fuck." *Almost there.*

As though sensing my thoughts, he halted. "And?" he prompted insolently, as though he knew full well what he was and reveled in it.

My heartbeat grew heavier, louder. If I could just catch him off guard... We almost never spoke like this. He wasn't paying as much attention as he usually did. He wasn't surrounded by thugs and demi-gods.

"And a coward who runs from any fight that's too hard."

The skin tightened around his mouth and his square jaw

hardened. My blood chilled. That look had preceded withering attacks before. Flashes of torture ran through my mind that I hadn't thought about in years.

Then he tilted his head to the side like a snake watching its prey. "Say that to me again."

"You."

He stepped forward.

"Are."

He adjusted his grip on Bloodbringer, battle-ready.

"A."

I made sure to lock eyes with him, not looking down at my hands. At those knives forged of elements he couldn't control.

"Coward."

We raised our blades at the same time. When we were young, whenever he got flustered, his accuracy dropped in favor of force. Some things never changed. His aim was a little off.

Mine wasn't. Mother would be proud.

I pressed the blade straight through his neck and used a burst of air to hurl him to the ground, pinning him there.

"Not so nice on the other side," I said, kicking Bloodbringer away and kneeling on his chest.

This kind of pain wasn't one he enjoyed. I ground the dagger in further. He wouldn't be able to speak for days.

I paused, considering whether to say the words I felt rising in my throat. But I wasn't one for tact. "This one's for Tyr."

❧ 28 ❧

TYR

Where was she? How could she skim me away like a child getting in the way? I fought Ares too. I wanted to feel the bite of my ax in his flesh. My mangled ax.

Together we could have overpowered him. Bellona's ferocity made me believe we could win and then suddenly...

I roared and pounded the table. With no idea where she'd gone, I couldn't follow. Not in the state I was in. Even now, my eyesight grew blurry from blood loss.

Could Bellona defeat him alone?

Against any other opponent, the question wouldn't even surface. Of course she could. Armies would bow at her whim. But Ares? He was the original god of war, a monster who'd mutilated half the gods in my kingdom single-handedly.

What if he did the same to her? Helplessness overwhelmed me. The vision of her in the same disemboweled state as the others brought vomit rising to the back of my throat.

I'd go out to help her. I'd...

I wavered on my feet. "Fuck," I breathed. Then again, louder. I was a liability like this. She was right.

Gathering my scattered wits, I headed for the bedroom, leaving a red trail in my wake. With hurried strokes, I ripped the blanket into strips. Less bleeding meant more focus and less chance of passing out. Movement hurt. Pain built as though it had been waiting for its time to strike. By the time I managed to tie the binding, cold sweat coated my skin.

With no one to turn to and no way to help, I raised a prayer to the divine. I had to believe that Bellona would be victorious. Of course she would. She was unstoppable.

I swallowed thickly, willing myself to believe it. I ached to fight with her. Even with my injury, my blurring vision, my shaking hands, I wanted to stand beside her, offer what help I could, hack the fucker to pieces.

But I could only wait.

No. I could do more. On unsteady legs, I moved to the door. Fen greeted me when I opened it, licking off some of the blood with a harried level of concern. My back throbbed and my limbs moved like a wooden puppet's, but I made my way slowly to the home where Hild was staying. If Ares had soldiers or started burning the village or came to kill her to spite me, the least I could do was defend her. The friend who had defended me so many times, not only as patrollers together, but after I ascended to godhood too. She'd lost friends siding with me.

I squinted at the road. This damn injury... Action helped the bubbling worry from surfacing. The worry that somehow, Bellona wouldn't be able to...

At the sight of the house where we'd left Hild after the

mob attack, my knees nearly buckled with relief. I hadn't remembered it being such a long way.

I didn't bother knocking on the door. I just stood guard outside with Fen sitting beside me.

"Tyr?"

It had taken Hild all of a minute to notice me there. So much for not worrying her.

At her side stood the woman who owned the house, Hild's late wife's cousin. They both looked at me like I was a vengeful ghost.

I waved, earning a fierce frown from Hild.

"You're hurt!" she exclaimed. "What happened to you?" When I didn't answer right away, she huffed and beckoned me inside. "Let me fix that. You look ridiculous."

"I thought you"—I winced—"liked the way I look."

"Not when you're carved up like venison." Her tone was terse but she reached for my hand, taking it gently to guide me inside.

The cousin moved out of the way. I hadn't learned her name, only her relationship to Hild's family.

Once Hild had sat me down in a chair and was halfway through re-binding my wound, she asked again, "Who did this to you?" This time, her voice wasn't sharp, but almost afraid.

"Hild..."

"It wasn't her, was it?"

"No, no."

"I can't fight like I used to, but I know a couple recipes for poison—"

"Hild." I sighed, meeting her eyes. With me sitting and her standing, we could look face to face. "It's... It's Ares."

Her pale face went bluish white with terror. I immediately regretted telling her the truth.

"So please, hurry up so I can go back outside. I'll protect you in case..."

But I just kept making things worse. All my efforts to protect her and the rest of Urd ended in disaster. I ran a hand down my face so I didn't have to look at her.

She rallied, her busy hands moving again to tighten my wrappings. "Hurry up? That's all you can say?" she muttered.

"Thank you." I was actually feeling a little steadier. "I'm sorry."

"You're injured," she declared suddenly.

I raised an eyebrow. That much was obvious. My hands and torso were stained with blood and I had a massive cut down my back.

"You can't fight out there."

I glared. "Yes, I can."

"Bullshit." Her eyes sparkled with sad merriment. "If Ares is here, there's no stopping him. Not in your condition. Let's just stay together, hm?"

As I looked back at her, I felt like I was hovering at the end of the world, on that fateful day that would consume all the gods. In a moment, I would leave. Fighting was in my nature. I couldn't just sit while Ares burned our lives around us, not while Bellona faced this enemy on her own. But for now, bloody and bruised and covered in sweat, I drew Hild gently into my arms.

29

BELLONA

The blade to Ares' throat wouldn't incapacitate him for long. I didn't know what he did to increase his pain tolerance, but rumors said his methods exceeded even my constant training.

I had to get him back to Eriset, where the truce still held.

"You've done what you wanted," I hissed.

When he bared his teeth in a joyless smile, blood oozed through the gaps. Unholy. It said he hadn't accomplished everything. My comment about Tyr and his helping me in the Great Hall put a target on him next. There was no way in hell I'd let Ares close to Tyr again. The image of my brother bending over his prone form sent a fresh shock of horror through me.

The bonds I had with me were too weak to hold my brother. Without my generals and soldiers to help, I couldn't send him to the endless prison of the Far Realm.

I was a goddess. I should have been able to. But the island

lay too far away to travel in one leap and Ares was strong as a bear.

"You've made your point," I tried again, slowing drawing out the knife from where it lodged in his windpipe.

His next choking noise sounded like *Tyr*. I slashed his cheek reflexively, but that didn't dull the intensity of his gaze. I knew exactly what that gaze meant: *I've found a weakness. You won't know when I'll strike him, but when I do, it will be sudden and horrible and leave you devastated. And I'll be glad.*

Every line in his face radiated the threat.

I clawed my hand. My attack so far had been small punishment. If anyone deserved the fate he'd foisted on Hrafnir and the others, it was my brother. I raised my gauntleted fingers and—

Ares was gone. Disappeared again.

I roared. Seriously? He ran again?

There were only two places he was likely to go—back to his ship for medical attention or further inland to find Tyr.

I rose, chest heaving. He was always so slippery. Any time I had a chance to truly punish him for all the carnage he'd imposed on my people and now the gods of Urd, he escaped.

It was the matter of a thought to reach Tyr's house. I tore through the rooms. Drops of blood drew a clear path to the bedroom, but he wasn't there. My insides seized. Could Ares already have taken him and disappeared somewhere else where I couldn't find them?

No. Think. Think.

The blankets were torn. Bindings for the wound on his back? Probably. That meant he wouldn't bleed as freely when he moved around again.

Fen was gone. I exhaled. That meant that Tyr was gone too, but not spirited away from inside the house. If that had happened, Fen would still be outside.

Where had he gone? The answer emerged with the question.

I stepped through the air to the house were Hild was. Fen sat outside. My hammering heart began to slow. Maybe my brother had headed back to his ship after all. His threat would simmer until some other time. For now, we might get a reprieve.

I hurtled toward the door to yank it open. Locked.

I didn't knock. Instead, I materialized inside. My eyes took a second to adjust to the dimness. The smell of salt and onions coated the air, but the scent of blood was faint, a marked difference from everywhere else I'd been recently.

"Tyr!"

He appeared around a corner, fabric wound around his broad chest. One hand kept Hild shielded behind him.

"Bellona!" he exclaimed. "Is he here?"

"No." But I looked in all the darkened corners.

He advanced, leaving Hild to stand in the inner doorway. "You left me," he snarled. "I could have helped."

"You were losing too much blood." Even now, his face looked ghostly in the low light. "You were a liability."

He flexed his jaw. "Where is he now?"

"Heading back, I think." I didn't add that Tyr was in his sights now. He'd be a fool not to have already figured that out himself.

Relief washed over his fierce, handsome face. "For now."

"For now," I agreed.

Heading back, on a ship, without his army. The idea tugged at me, insistent. When else would I get the chance to find Ares so vulnerable? The injuries he sustained during our fight were sure to slow him down...

"Then let's get doctors to the Great Hall," Tyr said, cutting through my thoughts.

Behind him, Hild's eyes rounded. "You came to me before getting a doctor...?"

Tyr turned with a tired smirk. "Priorities. You wouldn't have been able to recover." He shrugged one big shoulder without a hint of remorse.

Hild's eyes flickered with an obvious mix of criticism and thanks.

This movement was too slow. My blood burned to appear on Ares' ship and finish what I started. So why wasn't I rushing there alone?

I eyed Tyr. He'd be all right.

No standing army... Fuck me. Either I confronted Ares by myself, not knowing how many people he brought with him on the ship, or I let him get out of range.

I had to take advantage of this rare opportunity. Ares was sailing away right now, and I couldn't let him rejoin his army, not when he was so close. If I could just get on the ship, finish the job I'd begun in the forest, cut him to ribbons and send him to the furthest reaches to endure pain all his days...

"Yes, get doctors," I said. "I'll take out Ares."

"Wait," Tyr snapped, "you said he was gone."

"Leaving. He's injured. I got him in the throat, but he won't be down long. I can still get to him if I hurry." *I think*. I'd make it happen. I was the fucking goddess of war, damn it.

The slight haze in Tyr's eyes began to lift, replaced with blazing fury. Now he understood better what I had been fighting against for longer than he'd been alive. "Not alone you're not."

If I brought him, Ares, filthy coward that he was, would attack Tyr first. Tyr was strong, very strong, not only physically but mentally, but he was hurt. I couldn't risk it.

"Yes, alone." I pointed to him. Tyr's recovery wedged almost as large in my thoughts as the fleeing ship. The faster he healed, the faster I could focus all my knife-sharp attention on beating my brother. "Doctors. I'll be back."

Before a protest could leave his mouth, I stepped through the air.

30

BELLONA

I pictured the red-sailed ship. How many on board? Ares must not have brought much of his army, since he attacked the Great Hall alone. No, he'd come here to gloat, to hurt me in a way that wouldn't get him banished to the Far Realm by our father. My vision blurred to red.

Red sails.

Red blood.

Red paint across his eyes.

When I emerged onto a hard surface again, something had a vice grip on my arm. I whirled. Tyr's rough hand squeezed my bicep. He fell forward a step when we landed belowdecks, sunlight slashing our faces through gaps in the creaking boards.

I tore away. "What are you doing?" I hissed.

"The fuck I'm going to let you take him on alone."

"I can handle this myself."

His intense gaze burned with the fire I felt in my chest. He wouldn't be left out of this fight. He pulled out his blunted ax in one fluid motion.

"Don't hold me back," I said.

"Never."

There was no time to tell him off, to say I wanted him to stay behind, to curse him for defying me. To scream that the pain in my chest felt different now because I had found the capability to be hurt again. Love sucked.

I took him in with one sweep down his tattooed body, flexed and ready and already coated in blood. "This way."

Ares' ships were much like mine. I knew where the doctor's quarters were.

Tyr and I slunk through the lower level, feeling the faint pitch of the waves beneath us, until we reached a small room at the end of a hall.

My brother had barely brought anyone to help him. Stupid of him, but he probably knew that all-out war with Urd might trigger our father's wrath. Ares knew how to stay clear of that line. Flaying open a host of gods—fine. Open war with a company of soldiers—not fine.

Gods, how I hated him.

I flexed fingers in their metal gauntlet and met Tyr's eyes again. Another mistake. He looked roguish and murderous and ready, and I wanted him near me in all my battles. Anyone who dared oppose us—who dared so much as to dull that glint in his eye—would meet a painful end.

Whatever heart I had, shriveled and violent, lived outside my body. In him.

His generous mouth curved in something that wasn't quite

a smirk or a snarl. An invitation to an aggressive partnership. A last word before a battle.

I nodded and we crashed inside.

Ares leapt from the bed where someone had been tending the tear in his throat. The doctor jumped back. I charged forward, Tyr at my side.

It was as if the blood on Ares' neck were just the juices from a hearty meal. He didn't seem weakened at all. But he didn't reach for a sword.

I realized what he was going to do at the same moment he began to change.

With a poisonous smile, Ares grew and shifted into a huge black snake. His coils unfolded, cramming the little room full of scaly, sinuous muscle. The doctor made a gasping sound from where he stood pinned against the wall by his massive body.

Tyr and I reached Ares at the same time, blades sinking into flesh. My knife hit an area to the right of the neck wound, still visible in this form.

The snake hissed and struck at me first—thank the divine. I rolled, anticipating him, but the room was so small that his long fangs nearly grazed my back.

We couldn't fight like this. The snake had too much bulk to be cut down the usual way. Unless we struck his eyes or inside his mouth, we wouldn't win.

"Out!" I cried.

Tyr actually listened. Good. This was the perfect time not to argue. Once he was out of the snake room, I tasted air in my lungs again.

We sped toward the upper decks, the heavy rasp of snakeskin slithering behind us. Each of Ares' breaths came out as a deep hiss. The very ship heaved under his weight as he chased us through the hallway, up the steps, and into the sunlight.

Tyr ran slower than I did because of his deep gash. The knowledge renewed my desire for bloody revenge, but also stabbed me through with panic. Tyr couldn't shift. He couldn't run. Against the snake that was my brother, he was only a liability. *Shit.* I had known this would happen.

"When I tell you to jump," I told him, "jump."

He gave me a curious, challenging look.

"Don't argue. Jump off the side. Ready?"

His eyebrows quirked in confusion, but he spread his legs in a defensive stance to face the snake just as it poured out of the too-small door toward us. The wooden frame cracked and split to make room for it. Its speed was terrifying.

But so was I.

I branched my arms upward and inhabited the form of a falcon again, shooting into the air above the masts.

Tyr gaped, blunted ax at the ready.

My brother's slitted eyes glittered as he caught sight of me, tiny compared to him. I let out a screech of challenge, pinning my wings to my sides and whizzing toward those unguarded eyes.

Ares reared up, as tall as the mast, growing larger to match the increased space. My sharp beak only hit muscle. An angry, violent hiss met my small attack. I flapped back, just out of reach.

Below us, Tyr looked miniscule compared to the snake, but I could see him staring at me, then back to Ares, deciding what to do. At least Ares was too distracted to attack with the metal ship railings. One power at a time.

A dribble of blood flowed from where I'd struck the serpent's neck. Ares was angry now. Good.

Ares struck, fangs flashing, but I rose higher and avoided him.

I relaxed the distance between us, glaring straight into his reptilian eyes. Even in this form, his flashed hatred. I cocked my head, taunting him. I was small, merely prey to a creature like that. Why couldn't he get me?

I flew a little higher, looked down at Tyr, and shrieked the command to jump. The sound came out animal, but the meaning wasn't hard to figure out.

He didn't move.

I released another falcon cry, louder this time.

Move, damn it!

Ares' bulk consumed most of the space on the main deck. He was twice as long as the ship itself. One fang was longer than Tyr was tall.

Tyr began running, not toward the railing, but toward Ares' body that bunched to strike.

My brother shot upward. Some of my feathers scattered in the speed of my escape, just past the highest mast. The snake's jaws widened, a striped path down his long throat beckoning me inside. For a split second, I considered diving in to rip through him from within.

A snarled hiss of rage as Tyr hacked away at the body of the snake. Ares pulled back, retracting in on himself. But not fast enough. His throat caught on the point of the mast.

Realizing what I'd made him do, his anger doubled and he

thrashed. I knew that feeling—being unable to shift because pain didn't allow me to focus. It was exactly what I'd planned.

But I hadn't planned for Tyr to still be on the deck.

A muscular black coil taller than Tyr flailed, sweeping him to the side. I dove down, but too late. Tyr, crushed by the weight of the snake, had been swept into the sea.

Not allowing myself to consider how hurt Tyr might be, I willed myself to shift back to my goddess form before diving after him.

Cold water closed over me. The creak and crack of the rolling ship snapped to silence. I opened my eyes in the churning water. Where was he?

A disturbance in the water surged me farther from the ship. The vessel was capsizing. Also part of the plan. The plan that didn't include losing Tyr.

Bubbles jiggled madly in my vision. I was getting nowhere this way.

I burst to the surface. Sound assaulted me and waves carried me along hills and valleys. Still no Tyr.

"Tyr!"

If Ares had actually crushed him... If he was sinking to the bottom of the ocean... Gods couldn't die, but they could languish, tortured, unable to recover, caught in a dying loop. And if I didn't get to Tyr, he might forever drown until someone else, centuries later, found him at the bottom of this ocean.

Galvanized, I lunged beneath the water, kicking frantically to gain more depth. Through the churning dark, I saw him. His bones looked intact. No more blood than he'd arrived with. But his short-cropped hair floated above a bowed head and arms that drifted at his sides. He was sinking.

Swimming hard, I finally reached him, grabbed his hand to drag his arm around my shoulders, and fought for the surface. How far down had I gone? The light above looked feeble, though it was daytime.

Come on, Tyr. Wake up and help me!

I'd meant for Ares to impale himself and destroy his own ship in the process. Ideally, *he* would endure perpetual drowning. That was at least as satisfying as sending him off to be punished in the Far Realm. But this?

I steeled myself, calling on all the metal in my veins and blackness in my heart to reach the air again. Spite was a great motivator.

With each kick, I repeated pleas and curses and mantras.

And then...

I took a huge, loud gasp of air as we broke the surface. Beside me, Tyr still hung limp for a few seconds as I composed myself enough to see Ares' ship on its side with a snake thrashing among its ruins like the tentacles of some enormous sea serpent. Good enough for now.

Returning my attention to Tyr, I shook him.

Nothing.

Slapped him across the face.

A stir, a spasm, and a vomit of water.

My shoulders rose in a sigh of honest relief. No, more than relief. Because he survived, so did I. I felt alive. It was as though water hadn't been wet before or his skin, tight against thick muscles, hadn't been warm. I wanted to hold him to me tight enough to break him.

"You didn't jump!" I cried above the splashing waves.

Water streamed down Tyr's stupidly handsome face. "Yeah," he scoffed. "And leave you alone with him."

"I had a plan." I looked pointedly at the mangled ship, floating further away from where we floated among the wreckage.

"To almost get eaten by a giant snake. I swear, Bellona..." His frustration didn't fully mask the pride I heard warming his accented voice. When his gaze held mine, it felt like magnets clicking together, unable to wrench away. "You could do that, and you only taught me how to hop home after my shifts?"

My smile showed my canines. "There's something to be said for an advantage."

His glare was wicked. "Show me next time."

"Assuming there's a next time."

His answer was merely a growl, low and masculine.

Something primal in me responded to it. "Thank me, at least, for saving you."

His green eyes had grown dark, hooded. I still hadn't released him. "I hate you a little, this arrogance. You're not my commander."

"Just your savior."

"Gods can't die."

For some reason, this back and forth made me want to cross my legs tight to tend to the delicious ache there. I throbbed to be touched, and his thick thighs were treading water right next to me. Still, I wasn't one to give in first.

"Only suffer," I shot back, gripping him more tightly with my gauntleted fingers as I traveled with him back to land.

31

BELLONA

Our silence as we crunched through the pine needles shouted louder than words. His house was nearly in sight.

"What?" I finally demanded.

"I'm pissed that you left me." He shot me a look but it wasn't full of anger. I saw heat.

"I saved you before that," I shot back. It felt like a confession.

"Goddess of war," he mused, watching the path before him. "Queen of bloodshed."

He met my gaze again. "Conqueror of cities."

Something fluttered in my chest. Actually fluttered.

His voice lowered into something gravelly and seductive. "I want to torture you. Just a little." He searched my face, maybe to see if I knew what he meant.

I did, and my body flushed warm.

"You're hurt," I countered.

"Healing."

He did already seem a better than when I'd seen him with Hild, even now, dripping with sea water. Nearly drowning had weakened him, but he'd recover quickly. Our slow pace catered to his need for a softer level of activity. Hopefully not for long.

"You left me," he repeated, but this time, a wicked smile made of pure temptation tugged on one side of his mouth.

"I did," I goaded. "And I'd do it again." Our gazes clashed in a delicious challenge. Tyr was the same kind of wrong as I was. The air between us crackled. I felt every particle of space separating us, charged with possibilities.

"I hate that you're stronger than I am," Tyr murmured beside me as we walked.

I merely smirked at him as he continued his quiet litany.

"I hate that you came here to conquer us."

We passed Fen, who lifted his head as we passed. Concern filled his wolfish eyes. The saliva glistening on his large fangs reminded me of Ares in his snake form. I shook off the comparison. My brother was gone for now, probably for a while. If I couldn't hack him to tiny pieces, the next best thing was to rest.

Tyr opened the door and closed it behind us, leaving Fen outside. "I hate that you left me." Alone in the main room, he crowded me, not stopping his slow walk but this time forcing me to face him. I walked backward toward the bedroom, not breaking eye contact. My skin tingled at the intensity in his gaze. "I hate the way you make me feel."

"I hate it too."

A small line formed between his brows at that.

"You shouldn't matter," I explained.

"But you do," he finished, as though he had started the sentence himself.

We'd reached the bedroom. Dripping water joined Tyr's blood pooling on the floor. He really was injured. Was this the time—?

"Give me the blanket," he said.

Curious, I obeyed. It was already mangled—half the size it had been before. The rest had been used to patch up the gash in his back.

Tyr tore it in long ripping strips, the muscles in his arms flexing as he destroyed it. I watched. It was hypnotic. His biceps bulging under the skin, the tattoos in his forearms sliding with the movement, his large hands firm and sure...

It only took him a minute to reduce the entire thing to ribbons. I had my guesses about his purpose, but didn't voice them.

"Down," he growled. He meant on the bed. His expression was an odd mix of calm and maniacal. He devoured the sight of me as I crawled to the center and lay on my back, taunting him. I watched his breathing grow more erratic, his eyes darker.

He reached out and slid the backup knife from the hair pulled back on top of my head. With a firm thrust of the knife into the wood of the bedpost, he said, "For later."

I want to torture you. Just a little.

I felt dizzy with desire, but Tyr took his time.

"Is part of the torture how slow you're moving?" I demanded.

"Yes. Do you trust me?"

I didn't want to, but I did. I'd let him do anything to me. I bared my teeth in response.

"Have you ever thought," he said, picking up one ropey length of blanket, "about tipping your teeth in silver to match your nails?" As he bent closer, apparently imagining sharper teeth, he reached his hand up my arm, strong, starting at the base and pulling upward along all my muscles to the wrist. The trail of his hand burned like a good stretch. My pulse beat hard between my legs. I needed more of him over more of me.

"Not the worst idea you've had," I replied, breathier than I meant it to be.

He heard the arousal in my tone and smiled crookedly, evilly. I felt a loop of cloth tighten around my wrist. Moving to the other side of the bed, he secured the other end to the bedpost. "You only get to wear one," he said, meaning my gauntlets.

I offered him my hand. The way he slipped off my metal fingertips had my body pleading for him to be ferocious. But he kept stalking around me, adjusting, undressing, binding, like a great cat tracking its prey. I gave no instructions. No demands. I surrendered completely to his plan. Because he had a plan.

Sometimes he crawled over me to get a better angle and I felt how rigid he was. *Enough with this,* I thought with enough desperation that it became anger. But I was fascinated. Minutes sailed by as he bound me at odd angles, stripped me from the waist. One arm was bound behind me, the other above my head. One rope lay across my neck, not around, but firm enough that I could feel it resting there. He pulled my leather vest up to my collarbone, exposing my midsection. Finally, he pulled my naked legs apart and bound those too.

He was enjoying this. Every rope, every movement proved he was in charge. I was totally at his mercy.

And I trusted him. He made me feel wild and dangerous, but also secure. Here was a decision I didn't have to make, a problem I didn't need to fix. Here, I could lay myself back in this web of bonds and he could command me, as long as he did it right. So far, Tyr showed he wasn't good at everything, but he gave a damn good fuck. And damn good advice. And damn impressive dedication. And... oh gods, I wanted him inside me.

He pried my knife from the bedpost now crisscrossed with fabric. "I hate so many things about you," he mused, testing the tip against his finger.

"Then punish me," I urged. I deserved it all, and I longed for him to finally get on with it already.

He draped himself across the bed toward me, increasing the tension on the ropes he touched. I inhaled a strangled laugh when I realized what he was doing. The blade's edge slanted idly against the base of my pert nipple. Arousal made every touch searing.

I caught him smiling at my reaction. He rotated the blade just slightly so I could feel the change in angle. With my arms and legs tied, I couldn't move away. The tension made me release an obscene noise.

"Yes," he breathed, his face close enough that I felt the heat of his breath on my breast. "You're a terrible, terrible goddess." He scraped the blade lightly upward. I gasped. "You want me to be worse, don't you? Say yes."

"Yes."

He sat up, straddled my bare waist, and directed the point downward into the very center of my nipple. Just hard enough to hurt, to tease. It was unbearable. My breath became bracing pants. It was good there were no blankets on the bed. I would have soaked them.

This was cruel. I couldn't squeeze my legs together, couldn't find relief.

He rolled his hips against me, but he wasn't sitting low enough. His erection strained against the fabric of his trousers, rubbing against my navel. The movement of my breasts stimulated the pleasure-pain of the knife's point. "Oh...!" I managed. Curses and pleas wanted to be shouted like demands but I couldn't get them out.

He freed me from the excruciating focus on that one point and I could take a breath. The blade glinted in his hand. "Tattoos are just needles with ink," he mused, "in and out. Like this."

And he was on me again, forearm braced against my throat as he regarded the expanse of skin above my heart. The knife lowered again, careful as a surgeon or a writer, in infinitesimal stabs. He knocked the top of the hilt with a knuckle while guiding the points across my skin. Never going in far, but enough to break the skin. He worked quickly, my air running out. How long would he go on like this? I needed him now. Fully naked and fully mine. But this foreplay, this danger, felt better than some sex I'd had. Than most sex I'd had.

I gulped in air when he released me. "What is it?" I said, hoarse.

"T," he answered, sitting up and pointing to his own chest. Above the bandages, his initial was scrawled small above his own heart like a rune. His expression turned from seductive and dreamy to defiant and uncertain. "Because you're mine. You're mine, Bellona."

I kept my grin at bay. "You can't own me."

"I can try."

"Then I own you too." I gestured with my chin. "Take off your clothes."

"And what?" he said, closing his fingers around my neck as he brought his face to mine. "Fuck you?"

I stuck out my tongue suggestively, barely reaching his lips. He lowered himself onto me and crushed me in a kiss. He tasted like sea water and warm liquor.

When we parted, he said, half-delirious, "Why do I care about you? Why do I want you this bad? Get out of my head." He shook my throat, but without true violence.

With that, he let go and frantically started undoing his pants. I knew it. His cock sprang out, rock hard.

His muttering continued. "It's because you're powerful and beautiful and maddening..." I let the words soak into my skin like the blood still caking my hands. Each descriptor poured out of him in a seductive beat. The longer the list became, the more intense the gestures to go with it. A pinch there, a slap there, a—*oh gods, oh gods*—finger there.

I was agony and anticipation, a living scream for all of Tyr to take all of me. My legs were already spread. He smacked the space between them and finally plunged in. Deep deep deep, roughly pulling the ropes around my ankles as he pressed in farther than comfort. I cried out, body alight.

"You're mine, Bellona." The words grated, possessive.

"Queen, I'll make you fall apart. I'll make you beg." He grunted with the force of his thrusts.

Helpless to his touch, I let my eyes roll back. His big hand pressed down on my chest.

"You," he panted, "are mine."

Seen and wanted. The combination was so potent that I almost came at the thought. That someone like Tyr wouldn't need me to change before wanting me—wanting me for more than sex—filled me with a brutal ache. One he rubbed and pressed with his body and his words.

He was watching me when I met his eyes again, staring with a fierce, worshipful determination. It was better even than a hand at my throat. It made me picture the two of us at the head of armies, unstoppable. An ax balanced perfectly in his fist, a knife in mine, both tall, imposing, sharing a glance that said we would win before we even began.

"Tyr." The word was surrender, and he heard it.

His passion and pace doubled. I was liquid heat. Flame. In throbbing ecstasy as he rode me hard.

It was too much. And not enough, not enough! My head craned back, throat exposed like prey, and I exploded in shards of sound and shuddering.

32

TYR

I was delirious. This day couldn't actually have happened. But proof was everywhere.

Saltwater mingling with the sweat on my skin from when I plunged into the sea.

A makeshift bandage across my torso to stem the bleeding on my back.

Blood embedded into my skin from the horror in the Great Hall.

Images of a grinning warrior turning into a giant black snake.

And Bellona, bound, naked, underneath me.

Tiny dots of blood made a T above her left breast. She loved it. She loved everything I'd done, even too injured to be as physical as I wanted to be. Even when I'd grabbed the knife.

Unbelievable.

Some of her braids had come undone during the fight with Ares. They lay uncoiling around her head like small snakes. The way she'd bested him, and the way she'd looked at me before the fight... For someone like me, there was nothing sexier.

Bellona, for all her infuriating arrogance, made me feel I wasn't completely alone. Someone else fought an endless fight. Someone else hated and loved violence. Someone else understood.

I hadn't thought it was possible. Hild had come closest to truly understanding me, but even she couldn't erase that sense that I was a freak, seeking justice but fantasizing about pain. Never fully accepted by humans or gods.

Until now.

I gazed down at Bellona. Most of the black paint had washed off her face in the ocean, leaving dirty gray streaks that leaked into the shaved sides of her head. She smiled like a predatory cat, still bound at awkward angles in the web I'd created. I had tried not to wrench anything out of place with the bonds, but only to hold her limbs in new ways.

"You're a menace," I said, rolling my hips. Our sex had loosened her, but she squeezed me again with those internal muscles. She was muscles everywhere. An immovable pillar until she wanted me to dominate her.

I'd already come once but the thought made me harder. Bellona was so ferocious. I never wanted a soft kind of love, but something exploratory and unpredictable with a partner who could understand my struggle firsthand. Something that could last longer than the transient lives of humans.

She urged me on, grinding against me as much as she could in her position. "But you..." She stopped to pant, leaning into the sensation of me pumping into her. I felt my face go slack with lust. "You need someone," she managed.

I was in no mood to protest, so I just hummed in my throat.

"Time..."

She wasn't making sense. Only the place where we joined made sense. That wet, hot pulse was all that existed.

"It will take time," she continued. "I'll go back, and then..." She shuddered and revealed her sweat-shined throat with a whimper. I wanted to bite it.

"And then I'll stay... uhgn... for a while."

I slowed. This time, our sex was softer, an echo of the violence and urgency from before. We'd been here so long that red lines peeked from beneath the ties at her wrists. Somehow, I knew she didn't mind.

"What are you talking about?" I asked.

"I'll stay until... the gods are... back... on their feet."

I had trouble concentrating around the panting and the feeling of being inside her. It was a sharp, hazy ecstasy. I forced myself to pause, to pull out so I could listen.

A line formed between her brows when I did, annoyance replaced by resigned understanding. "The gods are not well," she began.

The reminder doused my flaming lust to low embers. King Hrafnir and the others had been utterly eviscerated by Ares. A scene I hoped never to walk into again in all my eternal life. I nodded curtly for her to go on.

"They need to heal. Until then, I'll step in to get this kingdom into shape. You'll help me. I just need to arrange some things with Thenios first."

"Thenios, the God-King?" I clarified, amazed anew at Bellona's stature and connections.

"My father," she replied, deadpan. The idea didn't thrill her.

I blinked. "Arrange what?"

She gave me a keen glance.

I realized it at the same time. I'd asked about her arrangements with Thenios, not her declaration to assume authority over Urd. That part, I'd simply accepted.

"A continued truce in Eriset. Generals to report to me while I'm here," she answered. "Why, do you want a queen?"

I was tired from the day and from our sex, too tired to threaten her, but I suspected that was what she wanted. I merely looked down my nose at her. "What if I do?"

"You're smarter than you look."

"You like the way I look. I bet you wish your hand were free to touch all the ink on my body." I flicked one finger of her metal gauntlet before letting it settle. "I want a partner, not a queen," I admitted, resisting the urge to lie beside her to avoid seeing her expression, which would give away whether she agreed.

I hadn't meant to be so honest.

So there it was. The truth. My soul out there for her violent hands to shred.

"A partner," she echoed. I couldn't tell what she was thinking. Her gorgeous warrior's face had become shrouded. Sometimes I could tell what she was thinking, because she was war and I was justice. We overlapped.

I dug in. "Yes."

"Would you go to Eriset, after this is over?"

I didn't know exactly when "this" would be over. Did she

mean after the king recovered? But I found myself saying, "Yes."

"Set up order here, then send my fucking brother straight to Abaddon?"

I grinned. I couldn't help it. "Absolutely."

Her bare chest rose and fell more quickly again. "Get the paint."

Her comment took such a turn that I struggled to make sense of it. Then I remembered. My gift. The little jar of warpaint she'd given me hell about.

I rolled off her, legs a bit wobbly, and fetched the pot.

She ran her tongue seductively over her canines, where I'd suggested she add metal points. With those, she'd be even more of a predator. I'd like to see that.

"Put it on," she ordered.

"You're the one tied up," I teased.

"You know you bow to me."

I did. She was my goddess. I dipped my calloused finger in the paint and drew a thick, dark bar across her eyes, this time imbuing my movements with care instead of domination. Muscles in her face twitched as I worked as though unused to gentleness.

"Now down my chin."

I applied the color to her plump lower lip, dragging it down to her neck. When I was finished, she smiled, dark and conspiratorial.

"Now we're ready," she said, voice husky.

"For what?"

"To go to war together."

It was a promise. A yes. Even an apology for that outburst in the kitchen.

My chest felt full. How had I won the fiercest, most stunning goddess in the Eight Realms? No ally or lover compared.

I began to untie her. We had work to do.

"Not yet, Tyr." She lowered her voice to a whisper, the sharp edges softened to something almost vulnerable. "We'll start tomorrow."

I swallowed around a rock in my throat as I nodded. Why was I getting emotional? I cleared my throat, almost angry, and traced the line of her collarbone with my finger to ground myself.

Being with Bellona, immortal queen of war, wouldn't be easy. But it felt right, like pieces clicking together that couldn't be pulled apart.

Tomorrow, we'd begin righting two kingdoms together. Today, she wanted more of me. And I had some ideas.

EPILOGUE: BELLONA

I strode down the line of uniformed humans. They straightened their spines and raised their hands in salute as I passed. Their uniforms were green, like the patch in Tyr's house or the forest or his eyes.

It was only the beginning of an army, but not bad work for one year. Crimes had decreased since the formation of the unit. I suspected that had something to do with the swift wrath Tyr and I visited on any who broke the few rules of the kingdom.

"Left!" came Tyr's rich, authoritative voice. A few paces away from me, he towered above the line of men. He wore no uniform, but kept his signature look—stripped to the waist, brand new ax Tyrving at his belt (his last mangled one had been lost in the sea). Where his belt sagged from the weight of the ax, exposing the swell of his hip and the line disappearing beneath his waistline, was a new tattoo. Tucked among the tribal designs was a flame. My flame.

As one, the line pivoted away from me. Gods, I enjoyed watching people obey him.

"Three laps!" he ordered.

The soldiers sprinted away, single file.

At Tyr's side, Fen twitched to race after them. The Banewolf stood as high as Tyr's mid-chest now, bigger than any dog I'd seen in real life. Some days I wondered if he was a demi-god. Tyr spread his hand to stop Fen from pursuing them.

I met Tyr's eyes. He didn't smile, but there was a question in his look. *Sufficient?*

I quirked a brow to answer, *Almost.*

It would take more than a company of human soldiers to defeat Ares for good. My plan to skewer him on his own ship had worked for a while, but he'd eventually been found, returned to Eriset, and revived. Cytherea, of all people, noticed his absence first. The goddess of pleasure whose affair with Ares was an open secret. It was always some fucking thing or other. Only his eternal punishment in the Far Realm would satisfy my desire for victory and revenge, and, for the first time in decades, I thought it might be possible.

Generals brought me updates monthly. Thenios had miraculously kept his word about maintaining a truce until I returned, which gave me more incentive to stay in Urd. I couldn't stay forever, but for now, building an army with Tyr set my blood singing.

King Hrafnir and the others had almost fully recovered from the attack. Hild had made sure doctors went to assist their healing, despite the human-god divide. She was a good one.

Because of my command the past year, most accepted my leadership in their place and didn't defy me. Hrafnir returned to Varafjall two weeks ago. He wasn't happy, but pleasing people was never my strong suit.

Pleasing Tyr, on the other hand…

I approached him. The morning air clung to his skin and his hair, which had grown longer these past months.

"Three laps?" I asked.

"For you to observe," he said.

"If I'm evaluating fitness, it should have been eight."

"Then I'll make them run eight."

We slowly smiled at each other. Then he disappeared—I assumed to a different part of the pre-determined course to relay the change in orders—before reappearing. Fen snuffed in surprise when he returned. Tyr patted his furry side absently.

"Get in the watch station," he said, flicking his gaze to the small wooden structure there for housing supplies.

Eight laps. That should be just enough time.

Ever since Hild came to live with us—not because she was weak or old, she assured me—we snuck off more often so we didn't bother her. I enjoyed bothering people, but I liked Hild. She didn't need to hear our frenzied grunts and cries every night.

My pulse quickened as I obeyed him, slipping inside the dark space. A large, calloused hand wrapped around my neck, massaging, teasing the pressure points.

"You made me change my order," he growled, with no anger.

"It's my army," I replied.

I could just make out his smile in the dark. It was an

honest smile, happy, even as the air between us turned dangerous. He hadn't chosen to tip his canines with silver points, as
I had.

His tree-trunk thighs pressed against mine and my back hit
a wall. "You've been very bad." His breath played over my lips,
my neck.

"Of course I have," I whispered back. "I'm the goddess of
war."

"Queen of bloodshed."

"Conqueror of cities. And you"—his hands were at my hips
now, wrangling my clothes—"are the god of justice. Some say.
But I don't think—"

"Shut up," he murmured, distracted, amused, done with
talking.

"Make me."

Outside, the faint sound of soldiers on their second lap. By
the time the crunch of pine needles faded, Tyr was inside me,
harsh and commanding. Just as I liked it.

The building creaked around us—two gods in a fever of
lust. I wanted Tyr all over me, inside me, pressing and slapping
and squeezing in, becoming a place for me to call home. A
battle and a reprieve. Deeply known and always new.

I hadn't said the words and neither had he, but as time
stretched on, we both heard them in the confident walk of the
other, in the moments when we sharpened our blades together,
when we fought side by side, when we locked eyes above a
meal, and now, as he ground ruthlessly against me. The words
used to terrify me more than a blood-soaked battle. But Tyr
made them less terrifying. Inevitable. Not a threat, but a
promise not to let the other fight alone.

I love you. I love you. I love you.

THANK YOU!

Thank you for reading *Flame and Warpaint*! Please consider leaving a review. Reviews help authors like me get found by more readers.

Now, read on for a sneak peek of the next standalone Deathless Love story, a prequel novella, that will leave you begging for more...

Or, read *Wings and Blindness*—the Eros and Psyche remix that asks what would happen if Psyche were sent to kill Eros from the beginning. To get him alone, she'll have to bed him as his wife before she even sees his face.

This first book in the Deathless Love series welcomes you to the Eight Realms, where danger and desire lurk in every corner, and mythology isn't quite as you remember it.

Join the Foxy newsletter and read this book FREE!

The fight was not fair.

The new man stood a head taller than the sailor. He looked younger too—maybe thirty—with golden skin and dark hair falling around his clean-shaven face. Even in this hot weather, he wore brown leather trousers and a leather shirt that fit him like armor, molding to his muscular chest and thick thighs. Leather sleeves reached down to his elbow. His forearms, veined and corded with muscle, were heavily scarred. Even his long fingers, not closed in a fist like his opponent's, had scrapes and callouses.

The sailor glared up. The newcomer looked down. As coiled as my attacker was, I couldn't believe he would win against this enemy with power emanating from every pore. His flashing eyes alternated between hatred and amusement. For a while, no one moved.

"Pay attention." That flashing, powerful gaze flicked to me.

My gut somersaulted.

Quicker than the eye, the new man lashed out. A kick. A punch. A crunch. And he was holding the man by his neck as he yowled in pain over his obviously broken leg.

"She didn't want to go with you," the stranger said simply.

"We didn't hurt her."

Another crunch. Another scream. "I could have hurt you worse too. Should I try?"

The man was blubbering now.

"I think so." Again, the newcomer looked at me. "Do you think so?"

I didn't answer. I had no proof this new person didn't want me all to himself after this was over.

"Now, what I should do is twist off your prick."

The man went sickly pale.

"But you're not worth the extra seconds." He let my attacker fall as he released him. "Go. Leave, or I'll do it."

The man limped away, dragging himself as fast as he could go, cursing as he went.

The second attacker's body lay still beside me. He hadn't moved since he was tossed away.

My knees pressed against my chest as I panted with terror, holding myself close. The tall newcomer turned his full focus on me. His attention lit up my body like the sun. Even if I had been in a busy street, I doubt I could have looked at anything else. His power and confidence and beauty sucked everything toward him like a whirlpool. Despite my fear, I doubted this man would be as crass as the others. He might have an ulterior motive for helping me—probably did—but something in me wanted to trust him. Stupid thought. I was a bug being lured into a flashy predator's mouth.

After looking at me for a beat longer, he exhaled. "I should have twisted off his prick."

He didn't come any closer, and my face relaxed. "You should have." My voice didn't sound like my own. It was too much breath and rasp.

The stranger laughed again, this time louder. Then his amusement faded, the lines around his steely eyes deepening.

I couldn't quite get over how handsome he was. No, that wasn't the word. He was power and temptation, good and evil mixed. His mouth made me think things I shouldn't, especially after what I'd just gone through. What was wrong with me?

"Did they hurt you?"

Yes, but I knew what he was asking. "Not yet."

He ran a hand through his thick hair. The movement showed off definition in his bicep even though he clearly wasn't trying. My stomach liquified at the sight. "Good," he said. "Or else I would have killed them both, slowly, in front of you, and enjoyed it."

Emotions surged through my blood at that. Part of me wanted to see it, wanted to see this huge, beautiful man taking pleasure in protecting me. It felt like a fantasy. Too good to be true. I bit my lip.

"You look like you just arrived," he said, more business-like now. Again, I knew instinctively that he was used to being followed, every order obeyed to the letter. "I did too. Can I walk you to where you're staying? Card isn't kind to women traveling alone."

I stood shakily to my feet. "I know."

The stranger backed out of the alley in three strides, freeing my way out. My feet itched to run, to hide, but somehow, being with this man felt safer than camping out in the hills somewhere.

"What's your name?" I asked, as I emerged back into the light.

"Leander." A dimple appeared in one of his cheeks as he looked down at me. Up close, he was even broader, like a shelter I could winter under until storms passed.

"Vilet," I replied.

"Vilet." His sinful mouth caressed the syllables, but I still felt no threat toward me. "Where are you staying, Vilet?"

I wanted to live in his rich voice, like the baked sugar bread of my youth. But I couldn't answer his question. "I'm hungry," I hedged. "Let's get something to eat."

"A drink?" he guessed.

I nodded. The past few minutes were too much for me to process. I wanted to drown my pain, all the layers of it, until I lay in oblivious darkness. If I did it with Leander, I'd be safe.

I couldn't say why I felt so certain. He'd fought off my attackers, broken them, but I knew it was foolish to put my trust in someone so quickly. My brother might trust him if he were here, but my best friend back home would bare her teeth skeptically and beg me to be careful.

I'd be careful. And I wasn't lying. I did need something to eat. My stomach felt practically sunken in after four days without food.

Leander and I were silent as we wove our way out of the docks and up a stone path into the hills. A building, asymmetrical to account for the slope, had a wooden sign swinging on an iron hook outside: The Shell and Lemon.

"Tavern," Leander explained as we went in.

The front room wasn't full. It was an odd time of the afternoon to eat, so only a few stragglers bent over their mugs or bread or soup. They all looked up at Leander. No one spared a glance for me. That small mercy made me warm to Leander more. If he had to, I had no doubt that he could fight off this entire room of people. I glanced at his body again as he lowered himself into a chair. Every move he made was so masculine, so self-assured without being cocky. It was an earned pride. It made me wonder about what else he could do with his hands...

"The Eros-suna are vicious in Card," he said in an undertone, snapping me out of my thoughts. "So what are you doing here?"

"Visiting family," I lied.

He grunted, tipping his mouth.

"You don't believe me?" I shouldn't have asked.

"I'm used to being lied to. I've gotten good at spotting when someone's doing it."

I swallowed, my pulse hitching up again.

"You don't have to tell me."

"What are *you* doing here?" I asked.

"Visiting family." His deep-set eyes gleamed. A muscle ticked in his jaw, daring me to call him out.

I stared at him, feeling bold, but ended up saying nothing.

"Town's a fucking mess," he said, calling over the innkeeper and ordering us two specials and two beers. "*Almost* makes me wish I were back home. I'm sorry you got caught up in everything."

"Can we not talk about it?"

When he returned my gaze again, I couldn't help but remember how he'd seen me exposed. Complicated feelings threaded through my chest. I'd left my undergarments in the alley and wore only my knee-length dress, soiled from the voyage.

"Of course," he said. "I understand having things you don't want to relive." He placed one hand on the table, giving me a full view of his lithe fingers. "Let's not talk about any of it, any of our past. I like the idea that you don't know me at all."

"And I like the idea that you don't know me."

That dimple appeared again. "No past. All right. Future. What do you want in the future?"

My eyes lowered to his mouth, then back up. But that idea was too dangerous, too reckless. Thinking became as difficult as walking through water with him around, all his magnetism presenting resistance. "To live a peaceful life." I shrugged.

"What does that mean?" The question didn't come out as someone else would have asked it. Behind the words there was bitterness and longing and true confusion, as if living in peace were a fairy tale that he could never enter.

His reaction exposed my similar feelings. I didn't want to tell him what a peaceful life meant to me, what I fantasized about. I hadn't told anyone my secret dreams. Dreams were luxurious, expensive, and paid for in grief when they didn't come true. If I didn't speak them aloud, I was allowed to keep them. I shrugged again.

Leander's attention flickered around the room before he said, "I want to get away, find a small island where no one lives, and move there with my closest people. No one would bother us. It would just be food and drink and talk and late nights under the stars. Time with someone... special, whenever they come along. Or lots of special people, if they want to come." His smile was wicked, and a little unsure.

It was the first trace of uncertainty I'd seen in him, and gods, if it didn't draw me in more.

Bug.

Predator.

This was an honest piece of him. Judging from his commanding presence, he wasn't the type to talk about his fantasies very often.

I gnawed my lip. He watched. My core grew molten. I squirmed a little in my dress. "I want ducks," I blurted.

This earned a hearty laugh. "Ducks?"

"Yes, and a pond far away from civilization. I'll learn to play the kithara and on summer nights, we'll catch fireflies." My voice caught. "My brother will live nearby with cattle. Every full moon we'll eat together—me, my brother, his family..." My voice trailed off.

Leander regarded me, dark eyes searching. "I want that for you."

"It's stupid." I brushed a rogue tear from my eye.

He caught my hand. Sparks ignited in my blood, licking up my entire arm. His rough hand engulfed mine in humid warmth. "It's not stupid at all."

Then, suddenly, he released me, as if he realized what kind of reaction I might have to being touched by a man again without being asked first.

"It's not stupid," he repeated. "Ducks are great."

"They are. With their little bills." Why did I feel so comfortable with Leander? His physique dripped violence. Those shoulders were brutal. Those pectoral muscles had been crafted with power in mind. I shouldn't let down my guard, but he coaxed me to relax like no one had in ages. He was a wall that could stop anyone from getting to me.

"Are you alone in this scenario?" he asked.

My skin zinged at the question. "No," I said carefully.

His lips twisted upward a fraction. "Let me guess. Duck wrangler? Bodyguard?"

A breathy laugh escaped my nose. "Exactly."

The food and drink arrived, smelling tangy and fishy. Leander and I tucked in without hesitation. We didn't talk until the food was gone and most of the beer consumed. Leander ate food efficiently, vigorously, just like he did everything else. Our relatively tender conversation seemed to break the norm for him. I would have bet all the money in my pocket that he'd never talked about how "ducks were great" before today.

The bubbles in the drink lightened my head immediately. "Why did you save me?" I hadn't planned to ask the question. When it spilled out, I was upset at myself for letting it happen. No past. Just future.

He looked up, dark eyes framed by dark brows. His gaze pinned me in place. "I wanted to do something good."

Disappointment settled in my middle. What had I expected? That he saw something magical in me?

He settled back in his chair and crossed his arms over his chest, almost contemplative. "I've done a lot of bad," he said, voice lowering, "and I'd rather do bad things to bad people. Those fuck-offs clearly deserved broken bones and you clearly deserved to watch."

My blood sang at the dominant undertones of his words, the confidence that he could overpower anyone if he merely decided to.

"It worked out," he said. "Any half-decent person would have done the same. Problem is, there aren't many of those in Card. Honestly"—he leaned forward, crowding against the small table—"it was a pleasure."

His voice slid against my skin like gently scratching fingernails. I shivered. "I don't have a place to stay tonight."

Another admission. I shouldn't have had the drink. Damn it, *one* beer shouldn't have had this much effect on me.

Leander's eyes flamed. The intensity, the *invitation* in them made me cross my legs hard to tend to the ache there. "The tavern has rooms," he said.

My breathing had grown choppy. I thought I could feel his heat from here. Unless I was seeing things, his gaze settled, heavy and sultry as a touch, on my lips, my neck, my breasts. This huge, powerful being wanted me.

"Where are you staying?" I asked.

"Wherever you want me," came his quick response.

I could hardly hear over the blood pumping through my chest. It wasn't even nightfall, but I needed to feel safe, to feel wanted, to be held, to be fucked, right now.

My movements had grown clumsy. "There's probably a room here," I said, rising to find the person who had served us. I froze. Did Aphriso use the same money? I should have known the answer, but education came second to work or service in Eriset, so I had no idea if all the Eight Realms used the same currency.

A shadow rose behind me, dwarfing me within it. Fingers tenderly caressed my shoulder, then traced down my arm to my elbow, the touch impossibly light. It only made me want more.

"Is there..." I spun to face him. His chest met my eyes. I craned up. He was so big he could swallow me whole. Need built between my legs. "Do you... have a room?"

His eyebrows twitched in a sort of acknowledgment, as though he understood my true question. "I do now."

The next few seconds were a blur. Money exchanged, following someone down a hall, getting a key, door closing us in. When the door clicked shut, everything came back into focus.

Me and Leander. In a room. By ourselves. And he was looking at me with pure sin in his gaze.

He blinked. "You sure?" he asked, husky and ready.

I laid a hand on his bicep. It was hard and warm under my palm. "In the field," I said, "with the ducks, I want *this* with someone who can keep me safe." It was one of the last hidden pieces of my heart. Love was something I couldn't afford for so many reasons, but something my soul and body craved anyway.

"I'll make it good for you," he promised.

No one had offered that before. They took, whether it was like in the alley today or with men I chose back home. Their needs were more important than mine. I was a vehicle for their pleasure. My body could get them off, and, while I tried to reach climax myself, reach that place in me that yearned for release, I never crested that wave before my partner's savage thrusts turned into a grunt of pleasure, a spurt of warmth, and it was over. At best, they thanked me.

"Show me," I breathed.

ORDER STORM AND SANCTUARY NOW!

READ MORE BY ZORA FOX

Fae and Shadow duology
> *End of the Forest*
> *Trapped by the Fae*

Deathless Love series
> *Wings and Blindness*
> *Flowers and the Far Realm*
> *Flame and Warpaint*
> *Storm and Sanctuary*
> *Full Moons and Vampires*
> *Temptation and Tridents*
> *Candle Wax and Sunlight*

Find all of Zora Fox's spicy fantasy romance titles on Amazon.